Nipples That Spit

Malika Micucci

Spider House Publishing

DEAREST READER,

This book is violent. There are buckets of blood within these pages, as well as graphic descriptions of violent situations.

It also has on-page depictions of sexual situations.

If that is your thing, by all means proceed. If not, stop here.

You've been warned. Enjoy!

Chapter 1

Sex and Ceiling Fans

Who the hell sleeps with a ceiling fan in the middle of February? In Rhode Island , no less, Samn McLeod thought.

She snuggled beneath a red cotton sheet, one leg curving out, speckled with gooseflesh from the top of her supple thigh to the tip of her bare foot. The sheet did its job in deterring the overhead breeze that Brad had insisted upon, but something had woken her and she couldn't go back to sleep.

"I can't sleep without the fan!" he'd said, incredulously, after Samn had returned from the bathroom, having brushed the lingering taste of Brad's semen from her teeth and tongue.

Samn and Brad had been dating for about four months, but she only stayed at his place about one night per week. "Distance makes the heart grow fonder" and all of that. They had sex every time she stayed, almost like it was expected. She didn't approve of expected sex. It made the deed feel far too much like a job, but she conceded each time because she enjoyed it, though at times, admittedly, she wished it was with someone other than Brad.

Another thing she didn't approve of: he always insisted on cumming in her mouth. Like, you're wearing a condom, sir. Just cum inside me like a normal person. But he always pulled his dick out of her at the last minute, tore the condom off with one fluid motion and stuffed it into her mouth just as the load was about to blow, Samn lying helpless on her back unable to avoid the pearlescent tonsil onslaught.

Samn didn't mind the taste of semen. She actually sort of liked it. It was dirty, but in a good way. She didn't, however, enjoy being *forced* to taste it, not to mention the taste being mingled with lingering latex and spermicide seasoning. And she for fuck's sake was not swallowing it as Brad often suggested.

The texture. Just no.

Samn sat with her bare back against the cold headboard and the sheet tucked firmly beneath her arms covering her breasts.

Brad snoozed next to her, snoring. He lay naked on top of the sheet, arms tucked beneath his head, relaxing in a kingly pose. His penis was hiding from the ceiling fan and had shriveled to roughly the size of her thumb. She held her thumb in front of her eye and measured it, one eye squinting, just to be sure.

Yep, roughly the size of my thumb.

Very little light spilled into the bedroom. Brad's apartment was on the third floor of his building, but the city splayed out before them. Samn pulled the sheet tighter still at the thought of the open curtains. Who knew who was watching?

As dim as the light was, Samn noticed something odd: four slender scratches on Brad's ribs and one long scratch on his upper thigh. She didn't recall those being there while they were having sex, and she felt like she would have noticed them, particularly the one on his upper thigh, while he was straddling her shoulders and jerking himself into her mouth. She was a little distracted at the time, yes, but that was a big fucking scratch.

Samn, in the tenure of her sexual exploits, had never been one to scratch, and luckily no one had ever requested such an action. Pain didn't turn her on, receiving nor inflicting it, so she was fairly sure the scratches didn't come from her.

She leaned over him and the sheet fell to her lap. Cold air rushed across her breasts and her entire body shivered. She quickly wrapped the sheet around her again. Holding the sheet with one hand, she used the other to caress the scratches on Brad's ribs. To her surprise, her fingers were red when she drew them back.

"Still bleeding?" she said. "At least they're not deep."

As much as Brad left to be desired as a lover, seeing him there, naked and rigid in the pale light, lit a desire deep within Samn. She weighed her options: go back to sleep or fuck Brad one more time on her own terms, unexpectedly. No doubt, she would get a shot in the mouth for her troubles, but it may just be worth it.

"Fuck it," she said, and took his flaccid penis deep into her mouth, twirling her tongue around the head and shaft, feeling it grow between her lips.

Brad woke and smiled down at her. He started to get up, but she stopped him and pushed him back to the mattress.

"Just lie still," she said. "This fuck is mine."

Chapter 2
Samn's Tit Problem

The sex was satisfying. In fact, it was more satisfying than any she'd had in quite some time. She initiated it and Brad just relaxed in his kingly position while she rode him hard, grinding her pelvis into his with an unexpected fervor.

In the heat of her passion, Samn had forgone the condom and pursued her first unprotected sexual encounter. Maybe it wasn't the smartest thing to do, but she had been monogamous with Brad for quite some time as he was to her, and she had been on birth control since the age of 16.

It'll be okay, she thought.

Occasionally, Brad would reach his hands forward and grind his palms into her breasts in opposing circular motions, squeeze giant handfuls of her ass. At one point, to Samn's astonishment, he even pressed the heel of his thumb into her clit and careened it back and forth, ensuing an uncontrollable, shuddering moan from Samn. This almost seemed selfless to her, as it was for her pleasure, and it was something he had never done before.

Sadly, even though Samn was on top of him for the duration of the fuck, Brad had somehow found a way to Houdini out from under her, mount her chest like she was a Clydesdale, plug his sopping cock into her mouth and blow a massive load onto her tongue and throat.

It was worth it, she thought, as she kissed him and left his apartment the next morning. If nothing else, her teeth would be among the healthiest in the city. Who else brushes three or four times per day?

The morning air was cold on Samn's face, so she turtled her face down into her woolen scarf. The sun was hiding behind dark gray clouds and there was still about two inches of snow on the ground. It was mornings like this that Samn wished she owned a vehicle.

She took fast-paced long strides to better warm herself and shorten the duration of her journey. Her apartment was only about a fifteen-minute walk from Brad's, so it was hardly worth paying for public transport, plus a little exercise never hurt anyone. Couple her morning travels with the more pleasurable exertions from the previous evening, and Samn's workout routine was bordering on the intense.

She passed the lake that bordered the park and it was still frozen solid. She was gazing at it as she walked, but suddenly she noticed a slight itch under her shirt. She scratched at it through her thick coat, and initially it satiated the discomfort.

Unfortunately, before the lake was even out of sight, the tingling itch was back, though more intense. She scratched at it harder, but this time, most likely due to the thickness of her winter wear or perhaps the persistence of the itch, it persisted despite her best efforts.

By the time she reached her apartment, she was practically at a jog. The coat needed to come off and the itch needed to be scratched. Desperately!

She fumbled with her keys, dropped them twice, but eventually clicked the lock to open her front door and rushed into the house, dropping her overnight bag haphazardly on the floor and shedding her coat behind her on her way to the bathroom. The coat fell into a lifeless pile on the hardwood of her hallway.

Without the coat, she was better able to pinpoint the cause and location of the incessant itch. It was coming from her right breast. She scratched at it, but the padding over her bra seemed intent, like her coat, to sell her efforts short. She lifted her shirt and slid her hand underneath the cup of the bra, using three fingernails to scratch. Relief was felt, but only for a moment. Upon ceasing to scratch, the itch flared up again almost instantly. She scratched again. And had the same result.

She shed her shirt and bra, letting them fall at her shoes, which were caked in snow that was melting into a large puddle in her bathroom floor.

She stood before the mirror, breasts exposed, and scratched fervently.

This can't be normal, she thought. Nightmarish visions of illnesses she didn't understand raced through her mind and she absentmindedly dug into the flesh of her breast.

She cupped her hand under her breast and lifted it high on her chest, almost as if pointing her nipple at the mirror. Upon closer examination, it was just her breast causing the discomfort. It was, to be exact, the nipple itself. It was slightly darker than the other and surrounded by reddened, puffy skin.

Panic ensued. She took the nipple between two fingers and pinched it. This helped ease the itching more than simply scratching, since it was pinpointed to the ground-zero location. She continued to twist and enjoy relief from the itch, though her mind still raced with worry.

Is it cancer? Is it an STD? Was Brad too rough with me?

It was none of that. Though in the long run, Samn would come to wish it was.

Samn didn't have to work that day, a bitter cold Sunday, so she lounged around her apartment braless, wearing just a T-shirt for easy scratching and pinching. As long as she was proactive in dealing with the itch, it didn't seem so bad. It was manageable.

Later that afternoon, she had plans to meet up with Mandy for dinner at their usual Sunday meeting spot: Cadlyn's Bar and Grill.

She left early, again hoping to avoid public transit. She wore her coat, but had forgone the bra for easy access to the cause of her itch. As long as she kept her coat on, no one would be none the wiser.

Despite leaving early, she arrived a few minutes late. Mandy was already sitting at a corner booth, sipping a decorative alcoholic beverage through a tiny straw.

Mandy was a pleasantly plump woman with auburn hair, almond-shaped eyes and a beauty mark on her left cheek. Samn had always been a bit jealous of Mandy's figure, feeling that she herself was far too skinny, but Mandy disagreed vigorously. Mandy felt she was a bit on the chubby side, but Samn envied her curves, the way her clothing clung to every dip and rise.

Mandy dangled one booted foot, sitting cross-legged when she saw Samn approaching.

"Hey, girl," she said. "What took you so long?"

"I've just had a strange day. That's all," Samn said, taking her place in the corner booth.

The restaurant was warm and smelled of a variety of succulent foods. The people around them generated a gentle hum of conversation as they enjoyed medium steaks, grilled chicken, poached fish and a variety of breads and veggies.

A waiter appeared within seconds and asked Samn what she would like to drink. She ordered a White Russian, quickly citing the reason as her odd and frustrating day.

"What exactly happened today?" Mandy said. "You don't typically drink at a party, much less at dinner."

"Well," she said, running a hand absentmindedly into her coat and massaging her nipple through her shirt. She crossed her legs and uncrossed them nervously.

Mandy, noticing her hand rubbing inside her shirt and her nervous manner, narrowed her eyes over her drink and said, "Are you okay?"

"Yes. I've just had this strange itchiness all day." She pulled her hand out of her coat, coming to a full realization that she had been touching herself in what some would consider an odd, even sexual manner, in public. Even if her hand was under the thick coat, people could still get the wrong idea, much like it appeared Mandy already had.

"Itchiness?" Mandy said. "Where?"

"Isn't it obvious?" Samn laughed. "On my nipple," she whispered.

"Your nipple?" Mandy chuckled. "That's weird. New bra lately? Maybe it's an allergy to something. New body wash?"

"No."

"New lotion?"

"No."

"Nothing?"

"Nothing."

Mandy contemplated her options.

"Was last night 'Brad night?'" she asked.

"Yes, but..."

"Everything go okay? Anything... ummm, new?"

"Well, sort of."

"Did he cum on your tits?" Mandy asked with a stern ah ha moment. "I read in Cosmo once that women can have all sorts of reactions to semen. This one girl in Nevada…"

"Ew, no!"

"Then what was new?" she asked.

"Nothing to do with my boobs," Samn said. "He always nibbles on them, but it feels good, and it's never caused any sort of reaction before."

"Then what?" Mandy asked, leaning forward, elbows on the table, her face cradled in the heels of her hands.

"I got to fuck him for a change."

"Darlin', are you feeling okay? You've fucked him before."

"I know that! I mean, I got to initiate. He was just lying there asleep and I just went for it. It was nice. Typically, I just feel like a fuck toy to him."

"Well, that is no way to feel. I'll give that ass a piece of my mind!"

"It's fine," Samn said. "I'm a big girl. I can handle it."

"Sounds to me like you already started handling it last night."

Samn laughed. "I suppose so. It was nice to be in charge for once."

"Sadly, I don't think that has anything to do with your tit problem."

"True," Samn said, going back to contemplating medical emergencies.

Chapter 3

Alone With the Irritated Nipple

Samn spent that night alone after an uncomfortable walk home in which she spent a large portion of time pinching at her nipple through her thick coat. At this point she was way past the point of giving a shit what any onlookers would think.

She sprawled on her bed under a thin sheet and removed her shirt. The cool night air in her apartment actually made the irritated nipple feel a little better, and it was much easier to scratch it with nothing in the way.

She stared at the ceiling as she twisted her right nipple between thumb and forefinger and thought, *having Brad around right now wouldn't be so bad. It would almost be like an automatic nipple scratcher, seeing as how he can't go 10 minutes without sucking, biting or grabbing my boobs.*

After an hour or so, sleep took over.

She woke around 3 AM. To her surprise, she experienced no discomfort. She looked down at her breast, illuminated by the faded orange glow of the lamp on her night stand. It was still slightly red, but strangely, a solitary trickle of blood was cascading from her nipple, down the round underside of her boob and onto her stomach.

She started upright and breathed heavy. She dabbed her fingers into the tiny trail of blood and they came away red. She quickly grabbed her phone and began to Google the issue.

She typed:

"itchy bleeding nipple female"

The search results yielded nothing of consequence. She found herself gasping for air. She placed a hand on her bare chest and drew in a deep breath, held it and then exhaled. After a few repetitions, she picked up her phone once more and started to call Mandy.

The phone rang once, twice, but before the third ring occurred, Samn heard something. It was the scuttling of tiny feet, like a rat on hardwood.

Absently dropping the phone from her ear, she placed her bare feet on the cold floor. The sound came again, this time louder, closer. Very slowly, she turned and knelt down to look under the bed.

At first, there was only darkness. Then she noticed a dark shadow moving, accompanied by the strange scuttling sound.

Eww, rats! she thought.

She backed away without taking her eyes off the tiny rodent. Suddenly, it started toward her, scraping its tiny claws across the floor and intensifying the terrible sound. The tiny legs of the beast worked hard and the scratches blended together to generate an odd humming noise.

She backed away again, but stopped when her leg bumped into her desk, the cold and the suddenness of the interruption ceased her movement. It was then that the tiny thing before her came into view.

It wasn't a rat, but a tiny humanoid being with purplish-gray skin. It had large, radial, yellow eyes that opened wide and held her in its vision. The thing stood about two inches tall with large, curving nails at the tips of each finger and toe. It opened its mouth and a bright red tongue unfolded and lolled out over a row of needle-sharp teeth.

The creature reared its head back and growled with volume that betrayed its tiny stature.

Samn couldn't believe what sat before her. What was it? She leapt to her feet and ran to the bedroom door, stopping in the hall and looking back into the bedroom. Her eyes widened with fear when she noticed that the thing was scurrying in her direction emitting a strange, guttural growl with each breath it drew into its tiny chest.

Samn turned and ran down the hall, but slipped on the long, hand-sewn rug her mother had made for her when she had first moved out. The rug folded like an accordion and sent Samn sliding down the hall, arms flailing, feet sliding and mouth screaming. She crashed into the tiny wooden table at the end of the hall and collapsed to the floor feeling intense pain in her hip and back.

She sat helpless at the end of the hall with her back against what was left of the tiny table. She remembered thinking numerous times, *I should move that rug. Someone is going to get hurt.*

And now she thought, *Damn it! I was right.*

The first thing that registered in her dazed mind were the eyes: wide and yellow, glowing, with tiny black dots for pupils. They emerged out of the darkness like a nightmare out of a dream.

Next, she saw the teeth, faded in the darkness of night, but still distinguishable as a row of dangerous fangs—like a zipper on a black hoodie. The face floated in the darkness for a moment like a demented Cheshire Cat. Then the body came into view.

Its arms were outstretched, a stance that said, *give me a hug.* However, the fingernails dancing at the ends of each finger suggested otherwise. It was now that Samn noticed this tiny creature only had four fingers on each hand, and therefore she assumed four toes on each foot.

The nails of each foot tapped the hardwood hallway with each step, a thrumming clack, then silence, then another.

Clack. Clack.

It came closer, drawing raw, raspy breaths.

Clack. Clack.

It was nearly upon her.

Clack.

Its tiny hand reached out to touch Samn's foot, only a few inches away now.

Clack.

She could feel heat radiating off of the thing. It was so close she anticipated the scratch that would break her skin.

Clack!

But her vision faded to black before the scratch came and she fell into the unknowing world of dreams. Strangely though, her mind still registered, even in her stress-induced dream state, the persistent clicking of sharp toenails and wooden floor.

Clack. Clack. Clack.

And then nothing.

When Samn woke, vibrant sunlight was streaming through the window at the end of the hall. Her back hurt. She twisted to see a large purple bruise, and then noticed she was still topless. She had spent the night in the hallway, facedown, breasts pressed against the hardwood floor.

It was then that she noticed her nipple was itching again. Only this time it was a painful itch, a nagging spot like an infected sore covered in flies. It looked swollen and the trickle of blood had dried. It flaked away when she scratched the nipple to ease the incessant itch.

She stood and drug herself to her bedroom, searching for signs of a tiny, purplish-gray monster as she went. When she found nothing, she felt incredibly stupid having allowed a dream to have such a profound effect on her.

Her body was stiff from spending the night on the floor, and cold from being laid bare for the majority of the night. She continued to scratch her nipple as she rummaged through her closet for something to wear. The decision was an important one. It had to be thick enough for warmth, yet thin enough for easy scratching.

She chose a teal, woolen sweater and slid it on after slipping her C-cups into a thin, satin bra. No extra padding. No push-up pads. Just minimal fabric for unhindered access to her irritated nipple.

Work was going to be interesting.

Chapter 4

The Subtle Art of Public Scratching

Samn showed up for work on time. She shed her thick, winter coat quickly, stashing it in the break room. The teal sweater hid her secret well, and to accompany it and complete her fashion for the day, she sported dark brown slacks and brown dress shoes. Her hair was combed back and pinned on the sides, hanging loosely about her shoulders.

Samn took her station in the "Women's Clothes" department, leaning against a kiosk by the changing rooms. She hunkered down and tucked her hand under her arm, using her thumb to massage the incessant itching that for the moment at least seemed to have confined itself to the very tip of her nipple.

Customers walked by, but very few spared her a glance. For that she was thankful. The ones who did only spared a moment and mostly consisted of young men whose gaze she didn't appreciate.

An older lady approached the kiosk and smiled. Samn stopped thumbing her nipple immediately and returned a warm greeting.

"Hello, ma'am! Can I help you with something?"

"Yes, darling," the lady said. "Do you know if you have this blouse in a medium? I've looked all over but didn't see one, but I admit my eyes aren't the best." She laughed.

This woman reminded Samn of her Aunt Marge. She had the same curly brown hair, streaked with gray, heavy lines around the eyes, and the wrong shade of pink lipstick, at least in Samn's humble opinion. Still, she was kind, just like Marge, and that mattered.

Samn smiled warmly, ignoring the insatiable itching, and said, "Right this way. I'll be happy to take a look."

Samn led the way through a maze of flowery dresses on hangers and pressed slacks folded neatly on tables. The blouse in question was on the back wall and Samn would be shocked if they didn't have a medium.

As she walked, her nipple itched incessantly. She fought the urge to scratch it, which stretched her customer service smile into an awkward grimace. She raised her hand, pretending to brush her hair back, and on the way back down gave the annoying nipple a rough clench between forefinger and thumb. She felt pain through sweater and bra and winced.

The pain faded quickly and the itching subsided. Samn's warm smile returned in force, so she turned to the woman and said, "Here we are. Now, let's take a look for that blouse. I'm sure we have one somewhere."

She hated her customer service voice. It sounded so unnatural. She couldn't help but feel a little fake. But that was the way of things. Go to work, be fake, get paid, go home. And don't forget to scratch the nipple when it itches, covertly when possible.

Samn started sifting through the blouses which hung in neat rows along the wall. Plenty of smalls, a few larges, but she didn't see a medium. There was a lot to go through though. She was sure the store had one hiding somewhere.

As Samn flipped through each shirt, staring carefully at each colorful size marker as she went, the itching returned in force. It came over her so suddenly that she reflexively started rubbing her breast.

"Are you ok, honey?" the woman said, tapping Samn's shoulder.

Samn turned to face her, still rubbing. Upon meeting the woman's eyes, she stopped, horrified.

"I'm so sorry," she said. "I just—"

"It ain't bothering me," the woman said. "They get sore, rub 'em. I've been guilty of it in the past."

Samn blushed and smiled.

"That's very kind of you," she said. "I've had a—"

Mid-sentence, the itching turned to a stabbing pain that paled her previous clench in comparison. Searing pain shot through the tip of her nipple. Samn grabbed her breast and screamed as she felt something wet fill her bra.

"Excuse me, ma'am," Samn said. "I'm going to run and see if we have that medium in the back."

"Are you ok, honey? You don't look so good."

"I'll be fine," Samn said, stumbling away awkwardly. "I'll be right back."

Samn clutched her breast and ran as fast as she could. She met the gray double doors that led into the building's storage area and exploded into the hallway. Two employees stood next to the doors chatting, so Samn whispered frustrations and obscenities as she continued down the hall and into the women's employee bathroom.

Once inside, she locked the door and ran to the mirror. She lifted her shirt and unfastened the C-cups supporting her breasts. The bra was soaked in blood—far more than before. Horrified, Samn looked in the mirror at her bare breasts to see a smear of blood trailing from her nipple and swelling along the bottom of her boob.

Samn lifted the afflicted breast and examined the nipple closely. At a glance, it looked normal aside from the blood, but upon comparing it to the normal nipple, she noticed a tiny hole on the damaged one.

"What the fuck is wrong with me?" Samn whispered.

The pain had subsided. It no longer stabbed, but had left behind a hot pain, sort of like the remnants of getting a body piercing. Samn had never pierced her nipple, but both of her ears were pierced twice along with her navel.

What pain was left was bearable and the itching had stopped, so Samn took a moment to dress and went back to work, making sure that no blood had seeped through her sweater. The woman was still by the blouses.

"I'm sorry about that," Samn said. "I was having some... difficulties."

"You may be pregnant," the woman said. "Tenderness in that area is common, you know."

Samn panicked slightly at the mention of the word. She couldn't imagine her life if she had Brad's baby. Nightmare! But then she remembered that everything was normal save for her nipple.

If she was pregnant, the thing had to be growing in her boob.

Chapter 5

Tuesday at Brad's

Samn leaned her chin in her hands, resting stomach down and ass up over the sofa, as Brad mumbled obscenities and repeatedly thrust himself into her. It felt good for a while, but she was so distracted by some of the shit he was saying that it ceased to be pleasurable.

Things like:

"Your ass looks like it's fresh from a Jell-O mold."

"Tell me I'm the king! The king of pussy pounding!"

And, "I think I just felt you cum!"

He was dead wrong.

His thrusts became slower and more prominent. The typical winding down before the male orgasm. She actually thought he was going to leave it in her this time and cum in the condom. At least she would be spared the oral finale, it seemed.

No sooner than the thought ran through her head, Brad withdrew from her vagina, turned her over with a tug of the hip, removed the condom and plugged her mouth, which was open to protest, with his moist dick.

It felt like it lasted an hour and that he came a gallon. She half expected it to start leaking from her nose. Samn wondered if an unsuspecting woman had ever drowned in semen. She would almost prefer to as opposed to suffering *this*.

Brad got up and fell back onto the couch breathing heavily. Samn didn't move, as though Brad was a T-Rex with a raging boner. She did not want to be seen.

After a moment, when Brad's erection had faded, Samn got up and started towards the bathroom.

"Come on, babe. Swallow it. Just once," he said, smacking her bare ass as she walked by.

She turned around and flipped him off with both hands. It was more dignified than trying to reply through a mouthful of spunk.

"We already did that!" Brad said laughing.

Samn picked up the pace and hurried into the bathroom and locked the door. She raised the toilet lid and spat the salty load into the water where it floated like a ghost. She quickly wiped her mouth and brushed her teeth, replacing the salty taste with cinnamon.

You can do better. You deserve better.

She walked back to the living room to find Brad still naked on the couch. He smiled at her and reached out his hand. She accepted it and he pulled her onto his lap. He kissed her lips, then neck, and then her left breast. As he started to nibble, she moved his head over to the right one.

The sensation was... interesting. He kissed and licked, which masked the sting with pleasure. When he started biting, it intensified the pain, but in a good way. He tried to start kissing her stomach but she stopped him, raising his head once again to the problematic breast.

"What the hell, babe?" Brad said, looking up at her like a newborn in the middle of breakfast.

"Just stay where you are," she moaned.

Brad continued tonguing and nibbling, then started down her stomach again. He passed her navel and Samn protested, thrusting her hips and pushing him aside. She stood and fumed at him oblivious to her nakedness.

"Damn it, Brad!" she screamed. "I need you to understand something. My body. My rules. Do what I fucking say, or don't do anything. You got it?"

She had never been so angry at him, and honestly couldn't remember ever telling him no. Not and actually standing her ground. But she grew angrier still when Brad started to laugh.

"What's so funny?" she said, feeling as though she were going to cry.

"You just look so damn cute, standing there all naked and pissed off."

Samn suddenly grew horribly aware of her nakedness and immediately tried covering herself with her hands as she looked for her clothes.

"No, no. Don't get dressed. We aren't done," Brad said, snatching her bra from her hands.

Samn snatched at it but Brad jerked it away, laughing. Samn pulled on her panties, pants and shirt as quickly as possible and then stood toe to toe with him. He dangled the bra above her head, laughing. Suddenly, his face grew grim.

"Woah, babe," he said, eyeing the bra with concern. "Is that blood?"

He lowered it to get a better look and Samn tore it from his hand and clutched it to her chest.

"Was that blood?" Brad said again, gesturing toward the garment.

Samn nodded and felt as if she were going to cry.

"What happened? Did someone hurt you?"

The sniveling asshole vanished, replaced by the guy she'd almost grown to love at one point. Sometimes she couldn't tell which one was the real Brad, or if both were. Some sort of Jekyll and Hyde personalities that tug-of-warred with the concepts of loving and using her.

She wanted to punch him in the face.

Instead, she cried and allowed Brad to fold his arms around her. She hated herself for doing it, but visions of blood, fear and pain ran through her mind and she didn't want to feel alone.

"No one hurt me," she said, "but I had an issue at work. It just started to hurt, and when I went to the bathroom to check, it was bleeding."

"Does it still hurt?" he said, using that tender voice she had grown accustomed to. She could never imagine that voice spouting the obscenities he mumbled during sex. The thought was absolutely ludicrous.

"Not as bad as it did, but yes." She hated how weak she sounded, like a child in need of care.

"Is that why you kept pulling me back?" Brad said, as though he'd just discovered the formula for time travel.

"Mmhmm."

That and other things. I'm tired of getting blasted in the mouth.

She wished she could say it. She wanted to say it. Maybe this could be a decent relationship with proper boundaries in place. She opened her mouth to speak, but when she met his eyes she lost her voice.

Something about him lorded over her and stole her nerve. Where was the furious girl snatching at the bra and screaming at him? She was nowhere to be found.

"I didn't know," he said. "I'm sorry. I was just playing."

"It's ok," she said. "I know. I was just so mad. And worried. I don't know what's wrong with me. I think I need to see a doctor."

Brad nodded. "Yeah, probably," he said. "But make sure it's a female one. You can't just go showing my goods to some random guy."

He smiled playfully and suddenly Samn had found the furious girl. She screamed from deep within her. She clawed at her throat and tried to get out. Samn opened her mouth, the gate which held her back, but all that came out was: "Of course not. A girl doctor it is."

Chapter 6
Night Terrors

Despite Brad's constant begging, Samn insisted on spending the night at her place. Sleepovers at Brad's usually consisted of even more sex than they'd already had, and Samn was getting tired of brushing her teeth. It felt like the enamel was wearing off.

All the lights were off when she arrived and it was just past 11pm. Her right nipple was on fire! She thumbed it anxiously, which seemed to help but only a little.

She took up the accordion rug, folded it and stored it in the closet, and then cleaned up what remained of the shattered table. She plopped down on the bed, took out her phone and searched the internet for "female doctor near me."

Before she dove into the results, she cast a cautious glance around the room, remembering that hideous face and sharp claws.

Get a grip, Samn! Just a dream.

But it was so real.

She shook off the dread, the tingle in her spine, and turned her attention to her phone.

An overwhelming number of results stared back. She skimmed through them, discovering that most were actually male gynecologists. And even though Brad was a dick, she had to admit she didn't love the idea of a man prowling around down there. She just didn't like *him* telling her what to do. In fact, his insistence made her want to do the opposite just to maintain some level of self-respect and autonomy.

She erased her previous search and replaced it with "doctors near me."

The search engine seemed to better understand this time. There were no gynecologists in the results, just general practitioners. The top result had the most reviews with an average of 4.7 stars. She clicked on the link and found a middle-aged man with glasses and fine brown beard staring back at her. His name was Joseph Sprake, MD.

Brad would die if I showed my tits to this guy, she thought.

She immediately bookmarked the page.

Samn thought about changing into an oversized T-shirt, but decided free was the way to be. She took off her shirt and pants and flung herself upon the bed wearing only panties. She closed her eyes, having already brushed her teeth at Brad's. The last thing she saw before falling asleep was three texts and eight missed calls, all from Brad. She ignored them, saving them for morning.

Unfortunately, morning had not arrived when she woke. It was still dark outside and her phone informed her that it was only 3:30am. She felt intense pain in her chest when she reached to turn on her bedside lamp. She sat back in bed and massaged the nipple, but the pain intensified.

She looked down and was met with a horrific sight. Her areola bulged and undulated, as though something writhed beneath the skin. She wanted to pinch it, but the pain was too great. She froze and stared as the tip of her breast danced wildly in the harsh lamplight.

The pain intensified further as the writhing slowed. The pain grew hot and sharp. It centralized on a single point, and Samn watched in horror as her nipple burst open and a tiny creature bounded out on short legs. Samn screamed as it perched upon the mound of her breast and stretched its arms, wiggling tiny, sharp claws at the ends of its fingers. Blood cascaded down her breast and her ruined nipple fell into a heap of flat, torn skin.

"You!" Samn screamed. "So, this is a dream."

But the pain intensified, mimicking reality.

The creature hissed in her face, and she felt its hot breath, which smelled like iron.

It was bigger than she remembered, about three inches tall. It rose from the gore of her ruined breast and stalked towards her, dripping and making tiny, bloodied footprints across her chest. Samn watched, frozen in fear, her body shaking. The creature reached her throat.

At first, she thought it would slash her with its claws, opening her throat, but instead it leaped from her body and walked across the bed, the tiny footprints fading to pink and eventually disappearing just before the creature jumped off the side of the bed.

Sam heard its nails clacking across the hardwood floor.

If this isn't a dream, I am so fucked.

Fear released her and she sat up in bed, causing a fresh gush of blood to rush from her nipple. She lifted the breast and stared at it, panicked. It still hurt, but nowhere near as badly as it had just before the creature burst forth.

She fingered the deflated nipple and winced. The nipple hung from her breast, wrinkled and mutilated. It reminded her of a used condom. Horrific thoughts rushed through Samn's head.

What would the healing process look like? Would this ever look normal again?

Would that thing come back?

Her hands shook harder at the thought. Surely, it couldn't climb inside the nipple again. Could it?

She pulled herself to the edge of the bed, clicked on the bedside lamp and surveyed the room with wide eyes. She saw no sign of the creature. Tiny blood droplets dotted the floor in varying sizes and receded into the shadows.

The thing could be anywhere by now.

She cupped her hand over the ruined nipple and tiptoed across the cold bedroom floor, down the hall and into the kitchen, where she located a large knife and slowly peaked her head back out.

She saw nothing in the darkened hallway.

Briefly, she considered leaving the apartment. She could go back to Brad's or perhaps to Mandy's, but the thought of running from her own home because of some three-inch monster sickened her. Besides, she had dealt with a few three, sometimes even four, inched monsters in the past.

Despite the levity of the situation, Samn chuckled at the thought of Brad's limp, shriveled dick cowered beneath the cool air of the ceiling fan.

Not quite a monster, she thought. *Snap out of it, Samn! This isn't the time!*

She stood upright and soreness reminded her of her wounded breast. She looked at the nipple, hanging flat like a deflated balloon on an otherwise perfect breast. Samn had never been conceited or thought too highly of herself, but the one thing that brought her confidence were her boobs. And now this little asshole had gone and fucked that up.

Anger rose up inside of her. She marched out into the hallway, head held high, knife held at the ready. She didn't even bother to tiptoe anymore. Instead, her bare footfalls thundered along the chilled hardwood.

She entered the bedroom and shouted, "Where are you?"

She heard it before she saw it: the same guttural growl from last night's dream.

Of course, am I dreaming again? I must be!

The thought brought a surge of courage as she searched the room for the source of the growl, which intensified with each passing second.

She felt sharp claws dig into her back as the creature landed on her from above. It dug in and clawed its way across her shoulder, then neck. It dropped and clung to her clavicle before sliding down her chest. It grabbed onto the ruined nipple and stared up at her with the same yellow eyes as before.

The claws piercing her areola brought a new kind of pain as they struggled to hold on. Samn drew back the knife and almost rammed it into her chest, but at the last moment, her sense of survival forbade it. Instead, she dropped the knife and started flipping at the tiny monster.

With each flip, the creature evaded masterfully, digging its claws into a fresh patch of skin each time. Samn winced but persisted.

"Hold still, you little bastard!" she screamed.

The creature pulled itself up and shoved its head back inside the ruined nipple. It wormed its way inside, pulling shoulders, arms and torso. Its legs dangled and flailed for a moment before it pulled them inside as well, and in a moment's time, Samn's nipple was whole again—a bit deformed, but at least it wasn't deflated.

Fear and pain quickly replaced any peace she felt at the restoration as the creature began to undulate and writhe beneath the skin. Searing pain shot through her chest and she clutched at her breast. She screamed and panic overtook her.

The writhing stopped and the boob stood still. Samn felt lightheaded.

Am I going to pass out?

Yes indeed.

Chapter 7

A Step-by-step Guide to Getting Rid of A Tit Monster

Samn woke the next morning, once again stiff from a night spent sleeping on the floor.

She sat up, shivered and stretched.

These dreams are going to be the death of me, she thought, but the thought was quickly undermined when she stood and saw the blood.

Her bed, sheets and pillow, were all soaked in blood. Tiny footprints trekked across the sheet and floor. Blood had pooled and dried along the floor.

She caught a glimpse of herself in the mirror above her dresser and gasped. She was nearly nude, wearing only panties, though she couldn't quite tell what color they were originally.

At the moment, they were red. Along with damn near everything else.

Dried blood streaked her torso, matted her hair and stained her panties. She looked as if she had just stepped out of an extra gory horror movie. Definitely something Italian. Possibly an Argento?

Lightheadedness threatened her once more, but she lurched forward and clutched the edge of the dresser. She locked eyes with the gory Samn in the mirror.

"Don't pass out," she said. "Hold it together."

But if the blood is real... THIS much blood, then that means that fucking monster is real too!

She cast a cautious glance at her boob, which at the moment appeared perhaps a little swollen, but overall normal compared to last night. She watched it intently, waiting for it to move, but it didn't.

But it hurt! It throbbed and itched, and when she scratched it, the throbbing intensified.

Samn began to cry, wondering what the hell was happening to her.

She almost called Brad, remembering how much better it felt when he was nibbling on the nipple yesterday. Ultimately, she decided it wasn't worth the cost—the cost most likely being a mouthful of jizz—and called Mandy instead.

The phone rang until Samn almost hung up, then a groggy Mandy mumbled an unintelligible, "hewwo?"

"Mandy! Wake up."

"Samn?" Somewhat more intelligible this time. "What are you doing calling me? My mom is the only one who calls me. Just text me like a normal person."

"Mandy, wake up," Samn whispered, almost as if the sound of her voice may reawaken the thing living in her boob. "I really need a friend right now."

"What?"

A little louder. "Mandy, I need you. Please wake up!"

"I didn't hear you."

"Wake the fuck up! Some fucking monster is living in my boob!"

"What the hell?" Mandy's voice rose to a crystal clear version of itself, all grogginess falling away. "What did you just say?"

"Something really strange is happening," Samn said, and felt tears brimming.

"Calm down, honey," Mandy said, her voice adopting a tender, maternal tone. "It's ok. Tell me what's going on. I heard something about a boob."

"You're going to think I'm crazy."

"No, I won't. Just tell me."

Samn lowered her voice once again. "There's some sort of monster living ... in my boob."

Silence.

Mandy chuckled. "You fucking bitch." The giggle became a cackle. "That's a good one. You scared the shit out of me! I'm going back to bed. Catch you later!"

"Mandy, I'm fucking serious," Samn shouted. "I'm scared to death. There's blood all over my bedroom."

"Did you say blood?"

"Yes! Mandy, please. Can you come over? I could really use a friend right now."

For a moment, Samn thought Mandy would hang up, convinced it was all a joke. Thankfully, she was wrong.

"Be there in fifteen."

Samn nervously paced her apartment from the bedroom door to the front door over and over again until Mandy arrived, taking extra care to keep the bedroom door closed and avoid it if possible. The sight of all that blood reminded her that this was really happening.

About 10 minutes into the longest 15 of her life, Samn's breast once again started to itch. When she scratched it, running manicured nails over the areola and taking the nipple between thumb and forefinger and rolling it back and forth, fresh pain pricked along the skin.

Samn lifted her shirt to search for blood, fearing that the thing inside was threatening to break out, but thankfully she found none.

When Mandy rang the doorbell, Samn sprinted to answer it, beckoning her inside.

"Ok," maternal Mandy said, noticing Samn was on the verge of hyperventilation, "let's take a breath. Calm down. Breathe."

Mandy held her at arm's length and coached her through breathing, and then drew her into a cozy hug—a much needed hug. After Samn calmed down, Mandy said, "Now, tell me all about it."

"How about I show you?"

Samn led Mandy to her bedroom, gave her an apologetic glance, and then opened the door. The room was somehow worse than she remembered. Several comparisons rushed through her mind: operating room, murder house, used maxi pad. The smell of iron threatened her with unconsciousness.

"Holy shit!" Mandy said, eyes wide and mouth agape. "What the fuck happened in here?"

Samn locked eyes with her. "Listen carefully, because I lose my sanity a little bit more every time I say it. There. Is. A. Monster. Living. In My. Tit!"

"You're dead serious about that?"

Samn started to cry again and Mandy wrapped her arms around her, her eyes distant as she processed the concept of "tit monster".

"Let's make a plan," Mandy said. "A step by step guide to ridding you of ... whatever this is."

Samn dried her eyes and nodded, tried forcing a smile.

"Step one," Mandy continued, "is to get this awful mess cleaned up." She gestured to the blood-soaked bedroom. "Then ... well, I never thought I'd say this, but I'll need to see your boobs."

Samn and Mandy went to work on the bedroom with a bucket of soapy water and a pack of magic erasers. After an hour of scrubbing and changing the sheets—Samn opted to throw the blood-soaked sheets away—the room looked good as new.

They sat upon the clean bed and Samn winced, rubbing the sore breast. She constantly struggled between allowing it to itch and scratching which caused fresh pain.

"May I see?" Mandy said.

Samn lifted her shirt, blushing slightly and exposing the right breast. The areola and nipple were once again swollen, red and irritated. Mandy poked the nipple with a single finger like starting a car with push-button ignition. Samn winced and withdrew.

"It's very tender. Please be gentle."

"Sorry!"

She rubbed two fingers around the edge of the areola, which hurt a bit, but Samn found it manageable. She watched Mandy's fingers get closer to the nipple, which hardened at her touch. Once hard, Samn could see tiny fissures in the surface.

"That is so weird!" Mandy said, examining the cracked nipple closer. "What exactly did this thing look like?"

"I don't know," Samn said. "Like a monster."

Mandy glanced up at her. "Come on! You can do better than that."

"It was about this big," Samn said, parting her forefinger and thumb about three inches. "It had sharp teeth and long fingernails. It was … purple, I think. But it was hard to tell with all the blood."

"You just described something out of one of those old horror flicks you love so much. You realize that, right?"

Did she just roll her eyes at me? No. No, she didn't. She's being amazing. And even if she did, let it go!

"I can't help what it sounds like. It's the truth!"

"I'm not saying it isn't," Mandy said, backing away slightly.

Samn started to feel very silly having such a conversation with her best friend with her tits out. Just as she was about to pull her shirt down, sharp pain shot through her nipple. She screamed and looked down and saw the skin writhing again.

"Did you see that?" Samn said.

"What the fuck was that?"

"I've been telling you! A fucking tit monster!"

"I thought you meant like maybe a parasite or something. Not a legit monster!"

"Well, now you know! When I say monster, I fucking mean monster!"

Pain shot through her chest again and she dropped to her knees clutching her breast. Mandy joined her and helped her pull her shirt down.

"Step by step," Mandy said. "We'll get rid of this thing. Whatever it is. Have you tried putting anything on it?"

Samn shook her head, trying not to cry. "What would I try?"

"Not sure," Mandy said. "What about peroxide?"

"Peroxide?" Samn said, eyes wide. "That sounds like it's going to hurt."

"Worse than having a tit monster?"

Samn rested on the floor holding the throbbed boob while Mandy rummaged through her bathroom cabinets.

"Are you sure you have peroxide in here?" Mandy said. "This place is a mess."

"Yes! It's under the sink."

Samn heard a cabinet door open in the bathroom followed by a loud crash, presumably of items falling from cabinet to floor.

"Fuck!" Mandy yelled.

"What was that?"

Mandy appeared in the bedroom doorway.

"I found the peroxide." She smiled, dangling the bottle by its cap.

As she approached Samn, screwing the lid off the bottle, Samn's pulse quickened. She had experienced peroxide on cuts, scrapes and more, but never on something as sensitive as a nipple. She imagined the searing pain and reflexively backed away.

"Calm down," Mandy said. "It can't be any worse than it already is, right?"

Samn raised her shirt once again as Mandy knelt next to her on the cold bedroom floor. Samn found herself unable to watch and instead locked eyes—well eye, seeing as how the creature only had one—with the Fulci Zombie poster on her wall. She waited for the sting, but it didn't come.

"What are you waiting for?" she said. "Just get it over with!"

Peroxide splashed onto her boob and filled every crevice of the damaged nipple. It stung, but Mandy was right. It was nowhere near as bad as the monster pain. In fact, the stinging seemed to replace the monster pain altogether.

Samn breathed an ill-timed sigh of relief, for as soon as she relaxed, the monster pain returned worse than ever. The areola and nipple undulated as the creature writhed inside. Samn looked on in horror, wanting to scream but unable to find her voice.

"What's happening?" Mandy said, her voice trembling, her hands shaking.

"It's … it's breaking out again!"

"What do I do? What should I do?" Mandy said, rising to her feet, hopping up and down and shaking her hands.

"Stop it!" Samn said. "Don't let it out!"

Mandy looked all around the room, searching for ideas, before settling on a pillow. She snatched the pillow from the bed and pushed Mandy onto her back. She placed the pillow over her boobs and applied pressure with both hands onto the right.

"Ugh! I can feel it moving through the pillow!" she said.

Samn gasped for air, gritted her teeth. Mandy applied pressure as the creature fought to get out through Samn's nipple, through the pillow, through Mandy's hands. But somehow, Mandy kept it in. After about ten minutes, the pain subsided and returned to being only a minor itch.

"I think it's ok now," Samn said.

Mandy got up and slowly removed the pillow. Samn's chest no longer moved, save for the rise and fall of her breathing.

"Maybe peroxide *was* a bad idea," Mandy said, her voice still trembling. "You need to see a professional."

"Like a doctor?"

"Not quite," Mandy said. "Get dressed. Grab your coat. I know someone who may be able to help."

Chapter 8

An Expert on Boob Monsters ... Sort Of

"Who is this guy again?" Samn said, hugging herself for warmth as she and Mandy walked down the steps to the subway. Thankfully, the steps nor the landing were very crowded, but the cold air was relentless, stinging her cheeks and ears.

"His name is Eddie, but people call him Spider," Mandy said, lowering her voice to a mysterious whisper.

"Spider?"

"It's a bit dramatic, but he's great. He's the only person I know who may know something about ... your problem." Mandy cupped both hands over her right breast as she said this and scrunched up her face. "He knows about all sorts of other paranormal stuff."

"I think this goes beyond paranormal," Samn said. "This could be medical. I could die!"

"If we take you to the hospital and tell them you have a monster living in her nipple, they're going to lock us up. At least, Spider will believe us. And who knows, maybe he's encountered something like this before."

Samn rolled her eyes.

"Just try to keep an open mind."

Samn followed Mandy onto the train and the door shut behind them. A wave of warm air rushed over them and Samn was thankful to be out of the cold, even if this particular subway car smelled a little odd.

The train lurched forward and jostled along the tracks while Samn sat in silence, her mind exploring all manner of pessimistic possibilities.

Will I have this thing in me for the rest of my life?

This thing is getting bigger. Will it eventually get so big that it bursts out and kills me?

Can we kill it before it kills me?

Does it even want me dead?

She closed her eyes and leaned back in her seat just as the train entered an ill-lit tunnel. Just as more thoughts threatened to present themselves, Mandy spoke.

"Have you told Brad about this?"

Samn opened her eyes and looked at her friend in the stale, underground lighting. She half expected a smug smile—though she had no reason to feel this way—but instead, Mandy wore a concerned look.

"I haven't," Samn said. "He definitely wouldn't understand. He'd probably just call me crazy."

"And *that's* why you deserve better than him!"

"Why because he wouldn't believe in a tit monster? Hell, I barely believe it myself and I saw the damned thing!"

"I believed it," Mandy said. "If he loves you, he should too."

The two girls locked eyes and Samn fought back tears.

"Thank you, by the way," Samn said. "I really didn't know who else to call."

"As Blondie once said, 'call me!'" Mandy sang the last two words, lifting an invisible microphone to her mouth and exaggerating each syllable. "'You can call me, call me anytime!"

"Fuck Blondie!" Samn said, laughing.

"It's good to see that smile again," Mandy said. "Oh, we're almost there!"

She stood and craned her neck as the train rolled to a stop.

"Yep, this is it! Come on. Let's go get your tit fixed."

Samn and Mandy ascended the stairs to street level and walked a few blocks in the stinging cold, past locations Samn was sure had to be the place, but weren't. They turned down an alley just as the sun began to set.

"Down here," Mandy said.

"Wait. How old were we when we met?"

Mandy turned to face her wearing a confused expression.

"I just want to make sure you're the real Mandy and not some imposter wearing her skin."

Samn shrugged innocently.

Mandy cackled, the foreign sound echoing in the otherwise quiet alley.

"You watch too many movies," Mandy said. She continued down the alley, hands tucked deeply into pockets. And then she said, "freshman year of college, student orientation. You were the dork in the ripped jeans and t-shirt nobody could read. You scared me a bit at first. Not going to lie."

Samn laughed and followed her deeper into the alley's darkness where the buildings blocked the sun and cast deep shadows.

"This is the place," Mandy said, gesturing towards a nondescript door that almost blended perfectly with the surrounding wall. She stepped up to the threshold and knocked three times.

They waited for a moment and when no one answered, Samn stepped forward and knocked twice. Mandy quickly added a third knock and looked at Samn, eyes wide.

"Spider only answers knocks of three," she said. "That's how he knows you're 'initiated.'" Mandy surrounded the word "initiated" with dramatic finger quotes.

"So, you are 'initiated?'" Samn said, adding mock finger quotes.

"I am," Mandy said with a mixture of pride and shame, which came across as a peculiar breed of uncertainty. "I saw Spider a while back for a spiritual reading."

"I didn't know you believed in stuff like this," Samn said.

"Well, I didn't back then. I was drunk, out with some friends, we thought it would be fun. One of my friends knew

Spider from a podcast and had visited him before. Let's just say, he made me a believer or I wouldn't have brought you here."

Samn opened her mouth to speak but before the words manifested the door opened and a pudgy man of about 30 years appeared before them. His arms, visible beneath the hem of a tight-fitting t-shirt, resembled a canvas covered in exquisite and macabre art, namely a large arachnid wrapped around each wrist. His shaved head and face were painted a ghastly white, and he wore heavy black eyeshadow. His intense gaze bore into them and Samn felt as if he could see her very soul.

"Three knocks were given," he said, his voice a hushed whisper, flailing his arms. "Spider comes!" When he hissed the word "comes," his hot breath produced a cloud of condensation, adding to his aura's mysteriousness.

"Hey Spider, cut the dramatics," Mandy said. "We have a problem we hope you can help with."

The mysterious and theatrical man disappeared, replaced by an average man. His posture shifted from stooped to straight, his intense gaze vanished and he pulled a pair of thick-rimmed glasses from his shirt pocket and placed them upon his face.

"Oh, hey Mandy," he said in a considerably higher voice and thick rural accent. "Get y'all's asses in out of the cold. It's cold enough to freeze hell out here!"

Spider's shop reeked of incense and marijuana. A black light lamp accentuated the white outlines of movie posters and the letters on a ouija board rug that stretched from desk to door. An electric space heater filled the tiny room with stifling warmth, causing sweat to bead on Samn's brow within seconds.

Spider plopped into a fluffy chair behind the desk and motioned to two chairs in front.

"Take a seat," he said. "Tell me what I can do for ya."

Mandy sat and urged Samn to do the same. Samn studied the room, surveying each curiosity carefully, wishing she had the balls to decorate her room in a similar fashion. She eased into the chair, almost missing it, unable to remove her eyes from human skull candle holders, creatures in glass jars floating in preserving liquid, and jack-o-lantern bowl filled with sweets, presented below a small sign which read "ALWAYS CHECK YOUR CANDY!"

"This is my friend, Samn," Mandy said. "She has an odd problem and you're the only one I can think of who may be able to help."

"Good to meet ya, Samn," Spider said, extending a hand.

Samn noticed his black nail polish as she shook it.

"What's your problem?" he added.

"Oh, I don't have a problem," Samn said, blushing.

"You don't?"

Mandy elbowed her in the shoulder.

"Snap out of it, girl," she said. "Tell him about your tit."

"Your tit?" Spider exclaimed, clapping his hands together. "Believe me, I'm flattered, but what led you to believe that I'm a tit expert?"

"Oh! That problem!" Samn said, snapping out of her stupor. "I have a…"

"Come on, out with it," Mandy whispered.

"I have a monster living in my boob." Her cheeks flushed from a combination of the tiny, heated room and embarrassment.

Spider placed his elbows upon the desk and steepled his fingers. His eyes met Samn's and he calmly said, "how long has this little fella been causin' ya problems?"

"That's the only question you have?" Samn said. "I expected you to laugh or maybe throw me out of here."

"A man in my line of work don't make no money not believin' people," Spider said, smiling. "Now, go on and tell me all about it."

"It's been a few days," Samn said. "It started out as an itch. A really bad itch that wouldn't go away no matter what I did. Then it started hurting. And twice now, the creature has actually… came out." Samn lowered her voice to a whisper.

"What was that? Came out?" Spider said.

"Yes, it burst through my nipple."

"What did it look like?"

Samn described the creature to Spider, recalling each detail from its toothy grin and purplish skin to its tiny stature and long, sharp nails.

"Did it try to hurt you?"

"It did hurt me!" Samn shouted, unzipping her coat, about to succumb to the stifling heat. "There was blood everywhere!"

"I'm sure there was," Spider said, "but did the creature mean to do it? Did it have ill intent?"

Samn considered this. She had no reason to believe that the creature actually wanted to hurt her. In all likelihood, it needed her warm body, her breast in particular, to thrive.

"I don't think so," she said, "but it's hard to say for sure. We didn't exactly have a conversation."

She fidgeted in her chair, trying to ignore the itching sensation beneath her bra.

"Would you please remove your top?" Spider said.

"What?" Samn said, her mind racing to Brad. He would throw a tantrum if he knew she showed her boob to this guy.

"It's nothin' weird," Spider said defensively. "But if I'm gonna help, I need to see the afflicted area." He spoke with a doctor's demeanor, but a farm boy's drawl. Samn actually found him a little cute despite the corpse paint.

"How do I know you're qualified to help?" Samn said, still not loving the idea of showing a stranger in a dark alley her tits.

"I have experience in this area," he said. "You suffer from a papillasite. A nasty little bugger that feeds on animal proteins and calcium. I doubt it'd hurt you, beyond the unintended consequences of bustin' outta your boob, but it probably peeks its head out once in a while to see if other food is around."

"A pap-a-what-now?" Mandy said.

"Boob parasite," Spider said. "In layman's terms."

"And you've dealt with these before?" Samn said, giving in to the urge to scratch and rubbing three fingers over the itching nipple.

"Dealt with them? Not personally, but I've coached a few ladies through it. But if I'm gonna be able to offer you any advice, I'm gonna need to see your titty. Just the itchy one," he said, pointing at her eager fingers. "Ain't no sense in pullin' 'em both out."

Samn drew hot breath into her lungs and released it slowly. Reluctantly, she removed her coat and grasped the hem of her shirt, but before she could lift it, Mandy placed a worried hand on her wrist.

"Are you sure you're comfortable with this?"

Samn nodded. "If it'll help me get better, I'd do just about anything."

She lifted her shirt above her right breast and pulled the bra down exposing the problematic nipple, which had grown puffy, the areola swelling around the actual nipple. Spider leaned forward and squinted, examining Samn's breast.

"May I?" he said, pointing at the nipple with thumb and forefinger.

"Do what you have to do," Samn stammered.

Spider pressed his fingers into the areola and grasped the nipple. He tugged it gently until the nipple was no longer crowded by the swollen breast. He released the nipple, which had grown erect in his fingers, and it receded back into the swelling.

"You have a fresh wound in the nipple," Spider said, peering down his nose and examining the breast from various angles. "How big was the creature the last time it showed itself?"

"Like I said earlier, about this big," Samn said, holding her hands about three inches apart.

"Oh, he's a big un!" Spider's eyes lit up. "Probably gonna get bigger too. He's probably in there clinging to the skin like a kid snuggled up to his favorite blanket."

Samn shuddered at the thought.

Spider squeezed the swollen areola and waited. When nothing happened, he squeezed the breast beyond the nipple.

"Does that hurt?"

"No worse than usual."

Samn met Spider's eyes and winced as Spider squeezed her breast once again, harder this time. Spider smiled. Just as Samn prepared a smile of her own, Spider said, "Found him!"

He withdrew his hand from her breast and he, Samn and Mandy watched as Samn's breast moved. The mound of her breast twitched and lurched. Samn screamed!

"It's coming out again!" she said.

"Oh no, it wouldn't dare," Spider said. "It knows I'm here. It can sense that I'll kick its little ass if it pops its head out."

"What's it doing then?" Samn said, watching the breast move. "It hurts!"

"It's tryin' to get comfortable again," Spider said. "All that squeezin' I was doin' disturbed his rest. Looks like it's grown since you seen him last."

The creature calmed and the breast ceased moving, Samn breathed a sigh of relief.

"You can put your shirt down now," Spider said, removing the glasses and leaning back in his fluffy chair.

Samn pulled her bra up and her shirt down, but left the coat off.

"I'm sorry to put you through the indignity of that, but please, think of me as a sort of doctor. I got no sexual pleasure from that, I assure you."

"None at all?" Samn said, looking at him sheepishly.

"Well, I didn't want to," he said. "But sometimes human nature is involuntary."

Samn blushed, recalling Spider's gentle touch and comparing it to Brad's uncaring groping. It was apples to Brad's oranges, and she had long longed for some apples and didn't even know it.

"Well, how do I get rid of this thing?" Samn said.

"It's simple," Spider said, "and it ain't. The simple part is killin' it. Catchin' it though, that's the hard part."

"What do you mean?" Mandy said. "If we kill it, isn't there a chance it may hurt Samn?"

"You gotta wait 'til it comes out," Spider said.

"I was afraid you were going to say that," Samn said, remembering the blood spatter that had stained most of her bedroom, the pain of the creature bursting out of her, clacking its claws and snapping its teeth.

"And these things can be fast. Fast like you wouldn't believe. So, when it comes out, you gotta have a plan and you gotta be ready. You catch it and you kill it." Spider performed a delicate chef's kiss motion. "And then, no more papillasite."

"And I'm left with a ruined boob," Samn said.

"It won't be pretty," Spider said. "I ain't gonna lie to ya. But it'll get better. And it beats the hell outta the alternative, which is lettin' that little fucker incubate and get bigger and bigger until... well, just use your imagination."

Samn collapsed into Mandy's arms and sobbed.

"I'm gonna be right there with you," Mandy said. "You don't have to deal with this alone."

"Umm," Spider said. "If you're gonna stay with her, you better be real, real careful. This thing doesn't need you. And it's probably hungry as hell."

Mandy laughed, but Spider's dreadful glare took the heart out of it. Her laugh sputtered like a dying engine.

"I'm not afraid of a three-inch monster," Mandy said. "It hurt my best friend. It better be afraid of me!"

"I just don't want you to get hurt," Spider said. "And it's probably closer to four inches now. And it's still gettin' bigger."

Chapter 9

Slumber Party Nipple Sitting

"Hey, bitch!" Mandy said, giggling. "Tell me, who am I?

She clutched her right breast, rolled her eyes, and exhaled a hot cloud into the chilled night. "Oh Spider! Examine me, baby!"

"Shut up!" Samn said. "It wasn't like that at all. I just want rid of this thing." But she found herself smiling, genuinely smiling, at the thought of his touch.

It had been a long time since she smiled and meant it.

"I thought you were going to suggest he latch his mouth onto your tit and suck the thing out. The way you were making eyes at him."

"That's fucking disgusting. And I was not!"

"What would Brad think," Mandy said, tapping her chin with her index finger.

"Seriously," Samn said and stopped to face Mandy, "Brad can never know about tonight."

"What? Like I'm ever going to talk to that asshole. Besides, it's your tit. Show it to whoever you want."

It is my tit, Samn thought. *I'll do what I want with it. And right now, I want to get the fucking demon out of it.*

They walked the cold night and took the subway back to Samn's place. Samn's nipple barely bothered her on the walk. Perhaps, the night air offered a numbing effect. If that were the case, Samn would rather sleep outside tonight just to get some rest.

Samn unlocked her apartment and the two girls walked inside. Mandy removed her gloves, coat and shoes and strode toward the sofa. Samn slowly removed her own garments, but as her body warmed, the itching began.

She walked to the sofa and sat down beside Mandy rubbing her nipple through her sweater.

"How about I'll nap now," Mandy said, "that way I'll be wide awake later. I'll sit right beside you while you sleep and if that little fucker shows his face... wham!"

She pounded her fist into an open hand.

"Sounds good," Samn said. "I probably won't go to bed for another couple hours."

"Alright. I'll turn in then. You have a night shirt I can borrow?"

Samn rummaged through her closet until she found an oversized t-shirt for Mandy: an XL Slayer shirt she'd accidentally ordered in the wrong size. Mandy slid out of her clothes and pulled on the Slayer T. It hugged her curvy frame and hung damn near to her knees like an inelegant sun dress featuring a fiery pentagram across her chest instead of sunflowers.

"You look hot," Samn said, laughing.

She watched a random horror movie, something she hadn't seen in hopes that it would keep her awake. She nodded off occasionally, but for the most part, the effort was successful.

The woman on the screen faced her fears with much more conviction than Samn. Samn cowered. She ran to friends for help. This woman, Isabelle, never trembled, never panicked. She hunted demons; they didn't hunt her.

Maybe I can be like that. After all, Mandy and I are planning to kill that little fucker tonight.

Isabelle died in the end, but she took the demons with her in a fiery blast. That's after she cut, poked and maimed the poor bastards.

Samn surveyed her apartment: walls painted gray with black trim, blood red plush sofa, framed posters of eyeless zombies, art-deco blood spatter, hanged women, and all manner of other phantoms lined the walls. Her music, her movies, her books, her lifestyle, all looked death in the eye and chuckled. And she shit her pants at the first sign of a tit monster.

Come on.

The credits rolled across the screen and Samn got up to go pee. She rounded the couch and screamed!

"Holy shit!" Mandy said. "You scared the fuck out of me."

"You're the one that crept in here on tip-toes. I didn't hear you coming. I nearly pissed myself!"

"Boo!" Mandy said, yawning. "It's nappy time, bitch. Go pee if you need to."

Samn rolled her eyes and trotted to the bathroom, did her business while scratching her nipple, and hurried back to the living room where Mandy had turned the TV from horror to sit-com reruns.

"I'm going to turn in now," Samn said. "What's the plan?"

"Well, you're gonna sleep. I'm gonna watch over you and if that thing shows up, I'm gonna kick its ass."

"I think you're taking this a little too lightly," Samn said, tears budding in her eyes. "I'm really scared, Mandy."

"Come here," Mandy said, and enveloped her in a warm hug, the oversized Slayer t-shirt acting as something between a robe and a blanket. "You're right. I'm just trying to cheer you up. I'm scared shitless, kid."

Samn met Mandy's eyes. "Let's make a plan."

Over the next 20 minutes, Samn and Mandy formulated multiple plots and hypothesized various outcomes, each one ending in a dead papillasite, and one of Mandy's featuring a naked Samn riding Spider's cock until he covered her in web.

"Shut the fuck up!" Samn said, smiling.

"You know you'd like it," Mandy said. "Now, let's just get that thing out of you so you and Spider can live happily ever after."

Samn rolled her eyes.

The final plan--the one they figured had the highest probability of success--consisted of a thick blanket and Samn's mini fridge from her last year as a college student before she dropped out and met Brad. Samn sleeps. Monster pops out of boob. Mandy wraps monster in thick blanket, chucks monster–blanket and all–into mini fridge.

Let the motherfucker freeze.

Samn settled into bed and closed her eyes. She took deep breaths but her hands trembled. Her phone buzzed on the nightstand. She lifted it and checked the screen.

Another missed call from Brad.

She put the phone back down and scooted to the center of the bed, clasped both hands across her stomach.

"Go on to sleep," Mandy said. "I got you."

Samn smiled and scratched her nipple one last time, and then sleep took her.

Samn woke to a familiar sharp pain in her right breast. She claimed her senses quickly and glared down at her nipple, the primary source of pain—but this time the entire boob hurt. It danced and writhed and tiny fists pushed and punched at the skin.

It's happening again, Samn thought, panicking.

Sweat streamed down her face and her eyes searched the room. Mandy stood over her, thick blanket in hand.

"Shh!" she whispered. "Try to lay still."

Mandy readied herself, a look of terror upon her face. The creature pushed against Samn's nipple and the torn skin flopped as it tried to break free. Blood ran from the nipple in a wide stream and cascaded down her breast, spilling onto Samn's stomach and then the sheets.

A clawed hand burst forth from the tip of Samn's nipple, wiggled its fingers and then plunged its nails into the mound of Samn's breast. Another hand followed, and the creature, using its hands and nails to clutch skin, heaved itself free, creating a larger split in Samn's boob. The papillasite, standing at about five and a half inches now by the looks of it, scampered across Samn's stomach leaving toenail scratches in her skin.

Samn sat up and felt faint. Blood oozed from her split breast as it hung limp from her chest, the nipple opened like a venus fly trap's mouth.

Mandy lunged at the creature, trying to wrap the blanket around it, but it nimbly leapt out of the way. It scampered across the mattress and jumped to the floor. Samn heard its toenails clacking against the floor as it retreated.

"Catch it, Mandy!" Samn cried. "I can't go through this again."

Mandy crawled over Samn and peered over the edge of the bed.

"I don't see it," she said. "But I see its footprints!"

Mandy eased onto the floor and followed the thing's bloody trail beneath Samn's dresser. She leaned forward, holding the blanket in front of her.

"It's gone," she said, but no sooner than the words had escaped her mouth, the papillasite lunged at her face, clawing and biting.

Mandy screamed and fell on her back, inadvertently releasing the blanket in the process. She tugged at the creature, but it had dug its claws into her cheeks. Blood raced down her face and filled her ears, matting her hair.

"Help me!" she screamed.

Samn forced herself to get up and placed her feet on the floor. Blood spilled from her lap and hit the hardwood with a heavy THAP!

She reeled and struggled to keep her legs beneath her. The room spun and her heart raced.

If I pass out, Mandy's dead.

Her thoughts raced back to Isabelle, the fictional heroine from the horror movie of which she had already forgotten the name.

What would Isabelle do? She wouldn't let some fucking monster kill her best friend. That's for damn sure. She'd kill that fucking thing even if it meant giving her own life!

She gritted her teeth and stumbled forward, snatching the creature by the nape of the neck. Carefully, she eased each of its hands off of Mandy's face and pulled the creature away.

She couldn't believe how strong it was!

The creature wiggled and writhed in her grasp, scratched at her hands and arms, roared in a guttural, gravelly voice.

Mandy sat up, leaking blood from her punctured face, and crawled toward the blanket. She grabbed it and wrapped it around the creature. Four tiny claws sprung forth from the fabric and sliced at it.

Mandy held the creature down and punched the papillasite several times, spouting obscenities each time her fist connected.

"You fucking. Little bastard. You ruined my face. You cunt!"

Her knuckles connected with the thing's face, but also the thing's claws, and blood ran from Mandy's hand. She didn't seem to mind.

"Open the fucking fridge!" she screamed.

Samn crawled toward the mini fridge and swung open the door. Mandy doubled the blanket over the creature as it fought to get out. She lifted it and flung the bundle at the mini fridge, unable to hold on for long. Claws pushed through the fabric with tremendous speed and at random intervals.

The blanket landed inside the empty fridge and Samn slammed the door shut.

"Don't let it break out!" Mandy said, mascara running like black tears.

Samn pushed the fridge over on its door and sat on top of it, and then she fainted, Isabelle no more.

Chapter 10
Papillasite Melee

Samn woke to the sound of Mandy's voice.

"We caught the fucking thing, but I'm not sure how to kill it."

A moment's silence, and then:

"She's hurt pretty bad. She passed out and hasn't woken up yet. She's lost a lot of blood."

Mandy paused.

"Just please get over here. I don't know what the fuck to do!"

Mandy hung up with an emphatic press of her thumb. She noticed Samn stirring and rushed to her side.

"Hey! Are you ok?" she said.

"How long was I out?" Samn sat up and the room whirled around her. She leaned to one side and caught herself on her elbow.

The surface is soft. Floor's not soft. Bed is soft. I must be in bed.

"About 15 minutes," Mandy said, checking her phone for the time. "I called Spider. He's coming over here to help us kill this fucking thing."

"Good." Samn swung her legs over the side of the bed, but Mandy stopped her.

"Woah!" she said. "Where do you think you're going?"

"I just want to make sure that thing is still locked up." Samn's words slurred together as she struggled to speak.

"It's still locked up. Don't worry about it. I'm more worried about your boob. That thing ripped you up good."

Samn looked down at her chest, which was heavily bandaged. Broad strips of gauze wrapped around her body and held her breasts flat with pressure, the bandage wet with blood on the right side.

"I did the best I could," Mandy said, shrugging. "I panicked and used all your gauze."

Samn laughed despite the throbbing in her chest. "That's what you're thinking about? Gauze?"

"I don't like to waste things! But I was panicked!" Mandy laughed too and hugged her friend. "I'm gonna take care of you. I promise!"

"I know you will," Samn said. "Never doubted it for a moment." Samn glanced at the fridge over Mandy's shoulder, still face down with books stacked on top of it. "That thing's being awfully quiet."

"Yeah, it hasn't moved in quite a while."

Samn released the embrace and stood using Mandy's shoulder to brace herself. They crept toward the fridge as if it were itself alive.

"Maybe it died," Mandy said. "If it needs to be inside a boob to live, that probably means it likes warmth, right? So maybe the cold killed it."

"Yeah? Or it's waiting inside to latch onto your face again once we open that door."

"That settles it," Mandy said. "We're leaving that fucker closed up until Spider gets here."

Samn and Mandy sat on the edge of the bed and suspiciously watched the fridge until a knock came at the door. Mandy stood to answer it, but Samn didn't let go. They walked arm in arm to the front door of Samn's apartment.

"Who is it?" Samn said.

"Pest control. Y'all had a complaint about a nipple critter?"

Samn opened the door. Spider stood on the doorstep, shivering, hugging himself.

"Come in," Samn said. "Quick. The thing is still in the fridge."

Spider walked inside and removed his beanie and coat. He walked further into the apartment and tossed them onto the couch.

"What happened to the face paint?" Samn said, just now noticing his handsome face.

"Darlin', they won't let me walk around like that in public." He roared with laughter. "Cops'd have a field day with my ass."

He wore blue jeans, boots and a black tank top with a small pentagram on the chest. A silver-studded belt held the pants to his tiny frame, and on each wrist he wore a leather bracelet: one spiked, the other holding a silver timepiece.

"Holy hell, girl," he said, leaning closer to Samn. "How bad is it?" He motioned to the bloody bandage concealing her right breast.

At this point, Samn noticed how close to topless she was and her cheeks flushed, nearly matching the bloodstains. She crossed her arms over her chest and said, "it's not too bad."

"She's fucking lying!" Mandy said. "That thing split her tit in half. Scared the shit out of me!"

Samn elbowed Mandy and shot her a venomous look.

"It's really not that bad," she said. "I mean, it's bad, but I'll live."

"Well, we won't let him back in there," Spider said, averting his eyes. "I'll stand in the corner while you put a shirt on if you want."

Holy shit! Samn thought. *A man offering to NOT look at my tits! So, they do exist.*

Mandy helped Samn to her closet since she still felt a little woozy. She picked out a t-shirt featuring Deep Red, her favorite Argento flick, and slid it on. Her chest stung and throbbed at the same time, but at least the thing wasn't in there anymore.

By the time they returned to the living room, the wooziness had subsided and Samn walked on her own, albeit slowly. Spider had kicked back on the couch with his eyes closed, legs crossed.

"Ok, let's kill this thing," Samn said.

Spider stood and pulled an e-cig from his pocket. "You mind?" he said. "For my nerves."

"Not at all," Samn said.

He took a long drag off the device and exhaled a vaporous cloud that smelled of cinnamon.

"Much better," he said. "Now, where is the thing?"

"We trapped it in a mini fridge," Mandy said. "It's in Samn's bedroom."

Spider's eyes grew wide. "Did you say fridge?"

"Yeah, we threw it inside and knocked it over on the door so it couldn't get back out."

"The fridge isn't plugged in, is it?" His voice trembled.

"Yeah," Mandy said. "On the way home, Samn said the itching was gone while we were outside in the cold, so we figured cold is bad for it. Maybe it would even kill it, ya know?"

"Fuck!" Spider shouted. "Fuck a duck with a cock-shaped saltine!"

"What's wrong?" Mandy said, shooting Samn a worried look.

"Cold won't kill it," Spider said. "But it will make it smaller. Much smaller. That's why they incubate in breasts: a nice, warm, soft place to grow. Plenty of nutrients. Close to the heart. Heat! Heat helps them grow. Cold shrinks them back down like a shriveled up pecker in an ice cold parking lot. How long's it been in there?"

"I don't know," Mandy said. "Maybe an hour?"

"Oh shit! We never will find that thing now. Not 'til it's back in your tit."

They checked the fridge and sure enough it was empty. Well, empty to their eyes. For all they knew, the papillasite could be right in front of them, but so small they'd never know it.

Chapter 11

Longing for a New Normal

"Why the hell have you been avoiding me?" Brad said with all the gusto of an entitled three-year-old.

Mistake. Mistake. Hang up now. Block his number. Delete him from social media.

But instead she said, "I haven't been avoiding you, baby. My phone hasn't been working right the last few days."

"Yeah. Ok," Brad said. "That's the lamest excuse I've ever heard. If you want to break up, just say so. I don't want to play these games."

She almost said it. Her mouth opened, each word clogged in her throat. She pushed. "I want to..."

She heard Brad gasp on the other end of the phone.

"Get dinner," she said, closing her eyes. "Tonight. It'll be great to see you."

"Just come over to my place. I'll order something."

She knew what she would get for dessert if she went to his place, and she'd yet to experience take out that went well with a sperm chaser.

"No, I want to go to dinner. Something romantic." Fear gripped her. She did it. She said no. She held her breath and waited for Brad to process the reply and offer one of his own.

"Yeah, ok baby. Sounds good. I'll pick you up at 8?"

"I doubt I'll be home," she said. "I'll meet you at Cherry's. Is that ok?"

Brad didn't answer right away. He sighed so that she almost felt his breath through the phone. "Yeah, babe. Whatever you want. Where you gonna be all day?"

"I have a doctor appointment and I'm not sure how long it will last. I may catch up with Mandy after."

"You getting that boob checked out? Has it gotten any better?"

"Yeah. In some ways it has, in some ways it hasn't."

"You find a good doctor?"

She read between the lines. What he meant was, "did you find a female doctor." Her mind drifted off to thoughts of Spider examining her breast, his tender touch coupled with his concern for her modesty. She wanted to blurt it out: "honey, a guy named Spider saw my boob, but just the right one. He also squeezed it. But it's ok. He was actually a big help."

Instead, she smiled and said, "Yep. Tons of good reviews online. Anyway, I gotta run. I'll see you tonight," and hung up the phone.

"On one hand: gag!" Mandy said. Samn knew she had been listening, pretending to sleep on the other side of her bubblegum bedroom. "On the other hand: you set some boundaries. Proud of you, girlie!"

"You're supposed to be asleep," Samn said, chucking a pillow at Mandy's face.

Mandy had insisted that Samn stay with her last night and she made a compelling case: Samn's apartment still looked like a crime scene, she was badly wounded and could use some looking after, that thing is most likely still in her apartment, and last but not least, she could use a friend. Mandy was right.

They had slept side-by-side and Mandy held her the entire night. Samn felt safe to be beside another human and not have to worry about a middle-of-the-night craving for a blowjob.

"Bitch, I sleep with one eye open. Isn't that what those metal guys say?" She mimicked guitar playing with her hands and mouth.

"Those guys are not metal. Not anymore. They're like expensive liquor that started out strong but some asshole added too much water over the years."

"That's the old Samn! Welcome back. How's your boob feeling?"

The waiting room smelled of lemon disinfectant and lavender. Samn arrived early, eager to get it over with, but the only difference it made was the location of her waiting.

Three other women waited, dangling crossed legs and browsing smartphones, their facial features accentuated by the stark artificial light of the windowless waiting room.

A middle-aged nurse, conventionally pretty, emerged from a large wooden door at the end of the hall and said, "Emma Stern." A woman on the other side of the room uncrossed her legs and stood, stuffing her phone into her pocket. The nurse said, "right this way, honey."

Samn waited and waited. Brad texted and texted. She didn't even read them, which birthed a pang of guilt, but her mind focused on other, more important, matters. She stuffed her phone into her purse, leaned her head back and closed her eyes.

Her breast ached. She considered going to the bathroom and removing the bandage, but figured she could tough it out a little longer. Thankfully, Mandy had offered to help her change the bandage before she left, and when last she looked, the fresh bandage had considerably fewer blood stains.

Minutes passed, felt like hours. The nurse re-emerged from the wooden door and in the same I'm-sorry-for-what's-about-to-happen-to-you voice said, "Samantha McLeod."

Samn made awkward eye contact with the nurse and smiled.

"Come on back. We're ready to see you."

The nurse held the door for Samn as she walked through. The disinfectant odor accosted Samn's senses like she had discovered the source of the infection--patient zero.

"Right this way," the nurse said, leading her down a long windowless hallway, each side containing wooden doors similar to the main entrance though not as wide. The nurse stopped in front of a door with a black plastic "12" featured prominently.

Samn smiled and strode inside and took a seat in one of the chairs sitting beside the exam table. She crossed her legs and waited for the nurse to punch whatever information into her tablet.

"What brings you in today, Samantha?" the nurse said, shifting her attention from tablet to patient.

"Please, call me Samn."

"Alright. Samn it is. What brings you in to see us today?"

Moment of truth, Samn thought.

"I'm...umm...having a problem with my breast," Samn mumbled.

"Oh dear. What sort of problem?"

"It's actually more of an--an injury."

"What happened?" the nurse tapped away at the tablet. Samn imagined the words she tapped: "abusive boyfriend/spouse."

"It's sort of hard to explain," Samn said.

"Please try. There's zero judgment here."

"I suffered an injury. It's torn up pretty bad, particularly the nipple."

"But what caused it?"

"I'd rather discuss this matter with the doctor if that's ok," Samn said, trying not to sound defensive but failing miserably.

The nurse stared at her for a moment, but then punched more information into the tablet and said, "very well. Doctor Sprake will be in shortly."

"Thank you," Samn said, but avoided the nurse's eyes.

Samn sat alone for several minutes, taking her phone out to pass the time, and then shoving it back into her purse once she saw the two dozen missed calls and text messages from Brad.

Boundaries, she thought. Setting boundaries is a good thing.

She settled into boredom until someone knocked at the door. Seconds later, a familiar-looking man entered the room, though the fine brown beard from his online photo was now a little longer and streaked with gray.

"Hello, Samn. I'm Doctor Sprake. My nurse tells me you're having some issues? What's going on?"

He sat down in the chair opposite her and propped himself up, elbows on knees. The man had terrible posture.

Samn decided to be matter-of-fact about it. "I've had an issue with my breast. I think there was some kind of parasite living in my nipple. Well, it busted out and left behind a gaping wound."

Doctor Sprake stared blankly at her. His face contorted to one of deep thought, and then he said, "can you please show me the wound?"

"Sure," Samn said, her thoughts inadvertently drifting to Brad, his missed calls and texts. Guilt washed over her, but she pushed it aside like a woman emerging from the shallow end of hypnotization. "But please keep an open mind. It looks horrible."

Samn lifted her shirt and started to unwrap the bandage. A little blood had seeped through the cloth. Doctor Sprake's eyes widened when he saw it, but Samn couldn't shake the feeling that the widening of the eyes was instead a product of lustful thought.

Again, she pushed the thought aside.

She cast the bandage aside and gazed down at her exposed right breast, the wound less fresh but just as gross. She made sure to keep her left breast covered, the reverse of a half-mangled individual who would typically conceal deformity while flaunting normalcy.

The breast tapered from her chest, starting round and working its way to an open point resembling quadrisected orange. The nipple exploded outward like a blown-out tire.

Doctor Sprake rummaged in a desk drawer and came away with a fresh box of latex gloves. He withdrew a pair from the box and snapped them into place on his hands.

"May I?" he said, eyeing the damaged breast with intrigue.

Samn nodded and fixed her eyes on the ceiling.

Doctor Sprake rolled his chair closer and leaned in and examined the maimed flesh with two gloved fingers. Even through the glove, his hands chilled her exposed skin.

"Have you ever had a nipple piercing?" he said, tracing the harsh lines of the wound.

"I have not," Samn said.

"I want to be honest with you," Doctor Sprake said, backing away from Samn and removing his gloves. "In all my years of medicine, I've never heard of a nipple parasite, especially not something that could do that. But you asked me to keep an open mind, so I will. I'll only say that I hope you'll repay my open mind and honesty with honesty of your own."

His eyes accused her of lying, but she felt he genuinely cared about her well-being.

"I know my story sounds crazy," Samn said. "I thought I was crazy for a long time. But I swear that every word I said is true."

"Very well," Doctor Sprake said. "Do you feel that whatever it was that caused this wound is out of your life now?"

Samn read between the lines. What he really meant was, "is the person who did this to you gone for good?"

"It is," Samn said. "I say that with certainty."

"Ok," Doctor Sprake said. "Let us focus on the wound and not the cause. I think we can treat the wound effectively with minimal scarring."

Samn breathed a sigh of relief. She dreaded a lengthy conversation about the plausibility of nipple monsters, and heaven forbid she utter the term "papillasite" to an actual MD.

"My team will be in shortly to treat the wound." He shot her a sympathetic and reassuring smile before exiting the room.

That could have gone worse.

Doctors and nurses spent about 30 minutes treating the exploded nipple. Samn kept her eyes shut while they cleaned and disinfected the wound, wincing at the familiar bite of dying germs in an unfamiliar place.

Instead of sutures, they used surgical glue to repair the wound. When finished, Samn peered down at the shiny breast to find it intact and mostly resembling its old self.

She left the doctor's office with about an hour to spare before her date with Brad. She rushed home and changed into a black dress, sleeveless but showing zero cleavage. She didn't want to take a chance on exposing the doctor's handy work and starting a conversation with Brad she didn't feel like having. She slid into comfortable flats, applied foundation, eyeliner and mascara, and even wore jewelry: her favorite dangly earrings and a black choker with a green medallion hanging in the center.

She looked in the mirror and smiled. She looked good and for the first time in a while, she felt normal.

She arrived at the restaurant 15 minutes early. A kind host showed her to the table where she waited patiently for Brad, who arrived 10 minutes late.

Samn had to give Brad credit. He cleaned up nicely. He wore pressed khakis with a blue button down tucked inside, black shoes and a belt to match. He had combed his straw-blonde hair back away from his forehead and had shaved all stubble from his cheeks and chin. This Brad reminded Samn why she found him attractive in the first place.

"Hey babe," he said. "Sorry I'm running a bit late. Not used to getting dressed up."

"That's ok," she said, smiling.

A waiter came by the table and handed them double-sided menus. Samn immediately ordered a glass of wine; Brad ordered a sweet tea.

"I'll give you some time to review the menu," the waiter said, and retreated to another table.

Samn glanced at the menu, but noticed Brad did not. His eyes focused on her.

"I've been scared, babe," he said. "The last time I saw you, you told me about some problem with your nipple, then you went MIA for a few days. Is everything ok?" He paused. "Are we ok?"

She didn't expect him to be so direct, almost vulnerable. She paused and gazed at the decorative tablecloth, thumbing its hem beneath the table. She considered his questions, weighed each response for ramifications, examined each path as though it could lead to a dangerous precipice.

"I'm fine now," she said. "I had a rough few days and some really weird shit happened, but I think things are better now."

Brad reached across the table, extending his hand. He gazed into her eyes and Samn found it difficult to believe that the owner of those doe eyes had ever plunged a raging boner into her mouth against her will. He had to know she didn't like it, right?

"I absolutely hate it when you cum in my mouth," Samn said, perhaps a little louder than intended. A man at the next table looked at her with raised eyebrows.

"What?" Brad said, pulling his concerned hand away. "What a fucked up thing to say at dinner."

"Well, it's true," Samn said, quieting her voice. "I really like you, Brad, but I haven't been super happy lately. There are some things about our relationship that I don't like and I thought it was only fair to tell you. That way we have our best shot at happiness. You know?"

"Oh my God," Brad said, burying his face in his hands. "Really? But you seemed so into it."

"How did I seem into it? Surely you notice me running to the bathroom to spit it out and brush my teeth every time."

"Well, if you don't want to swallow it, what else are you going to do? I never really thought that much about it to be honest. I remember the first time I did it, you really seemed into it."

Samn's mind rushed back to the first blowjob she'd ever given Brad. After a movie, sitting in the front seat of his Honda Accord, windows tinted. A million things went through her mind that night, but not once had she planned to suck his dick. He had pulled it out while they kissed. Truthfully, she didn't even see it until he was tenderly guiding her head toward it.

One moment, kiss kiss kiss.

The next moment, incoming dick.

She could have stopped, that's true. But it felt like he expected it, like it was a woman's duty after a romantic date to service the boner that she had obviously created. Completely fucked up mindset, in retrospect. Was it society that had trained her to believe such lies? Was it Brad and guys like him? Was it womanly intuition, peer pressure from dick-sucking friends? Too many possibilities. The past is the past.

Samn remembered Brad moaning towards climax and she thought, *what am I going to do*? Before she had time to even consider options, the first blast had landed on her tongue. She had started to back away but felt Brad's hand on the back of her head, not forcing her down, but suggesting. At least, that's how she interpreted it.

She had worked the shaft of his cock as he came, causing each blast to shoot harder and harder until she had successfully drained his balls. She'd looked up at him, lips pursed together as she removed his cock from her mouth, collecting each drop of semen on the way up. But that wasn't because she loved the semen, it was because she abhorred a mess.

A mess prevented is a mess you don't have to clean later.

"That was great, babe," Brad had said, leaning back in the driver's seat as he put little Brad away and buttoned his pants.

Samn had still opened the car door and spit Brad's spunk onto the pavement. Her first boyfriend had came in her mouth once and upon seeing her reaction had apologized profusely until she tired of hearing apologies.

Find a way forward, Samn thought. *Let the past die.*

"You're right," Samn said. "I can see how my actions made you think that. I'm sorry. I didn't want to be rude. I really liked you."

"Liked?" Brad said.

"Like!" Samn said.

"Why would you invite me to such a romantic dinner just to publicly accuse me of being a mouth rapist?" Brad stood up and Samn felt every eye in the room turn to their table.

"Brad, sit down!" she whispered, gazing about her peripheral. "Let's talk. Not shout. Talk."

Brad sat down and looked around the room as if only now realizing that they were the center of attention.

Samn leaned toward him and said, "I didn't plan for this to happen. I planned to come here and hopefully solve the problems that make me unhappy. That's one of them. I'm not accusing you of anything."

She reached her hand across the table, but Brad glared at it as if it were a poisonous snake.

"What else do you hate about me?" Brad said. "How else would you like me to change to fit your mold?"

"What? I'm not asking you to change. I'm asking you to respect my body enough to play by my rules." Samn sighed. "I love having sex with you. You are a beautiful, caring man, but sometimes when your dick comes out that man goes away. It's like you become someone else entirely."

Brad sat perfectly still. his eyes shifted from hers, to the table, to some unknown point in the room. Finally, he said, "I respect you. You tell me the rules and I'll follow them. I'm sorry, babe. I didn't know."

Samn smiled, stood and walked around the table. She leaned down and kissed him.

"That's all I've ever wanted."

Brad smiled back at her and squeezed her hand.

Samn heard clapping coming from behind her. She turned and saw a beaming middle-aged couple applauding and gazing romantically at her and Brad. Soon, other tables started to clap. Before long, the entire room burst into thunderous applause, as if Brad had just proposed and she'd accepted, not as if they'd just resolved an argument over cum shots.

She took her seat, cheeks budding with embarrassment. She and Brad ordered food, extravagant dishes neither of them could really afford, and good wine. They enjoyed pleasant conversation, avoiding uncomfortable topics for the most part, until the crowd in the restaurant started to thin.

"How long have we been here?" Samn said, noticing the near empty room and feeling slightly buzzed.

"Not entirely sure," Brad said. "This has been nice though. Thank you."

"Certainly. It was a fine idea, wasn't it?"

Samn took another sip of wine, draining what was left in the glass. She absently massaged her right breast, which felt plastic from the adhesive beneath her bra. Brad noticed.

"You said you got that checked out," he said, motioning to her breast. "What was wrong?"

"It was this weird thing living in there," she said. "This little monster. Scared the shit out of me."

Brad looked at her, mouth hanging open, like she had just confessed to an affair with aliens.

"What do you mean a little monster?" he pushed his wine glass away.

"This little creature about this big," Samn giggled, holding thumb and forefinger about three inches apart. "He ripped me up good."

"Ripped you up? Are you ok?" Brad sat rigid in his chair, fingers fidgeting with the silverware.

"Yeah, I'm ok now. The doctors patched me up after he busted out the last time."

Brad rubbed his eyes and smiled. "That's a lot to take in. Busted out? What does that even mean?" Angry Brad threatened to break out, destroying caring Brad like an itching nipple. Could she patch him up again?

Samn's smile vanished. She reached for clarity through the haze of wine.

"It means exactly what I just said. There was a little monster living in there and growing. Feeding off me. Spider helped us get it out and capture it, but..."

"Who the fuck is Spider?"

"Forget it," Samn said, leaning back in her chair, arms folded.

"Like hell I'll forget it. Who the fuck is Spider? Some dude helping with your imaginary tit monster. That's the worst excuse for cheating I've ever heard."

"Cheating? What the fuck? I never cheated on you!" Samn's voice echoed through the restaurant and the remaining people all looked up. She could feel their eyes on her.

"Hear me out!" Brad roared. "What I'm hearing is that you had some imaginary tit monster and you let some asshole named Spider get it out for you. Since that shit doesn't exist, I'm gonna assume you just wanted someone to feel you up." He calmed and leaned back in his chair. "Someone who wasn't me."

"It wasn't like that!" Samn shrieked, clutching the edge of the table in both hands. "That thing is fucking real! It nearly killed me. Just ask Mandy."

"Ask your bitch friend who hates me and would love to cover up for your lying ass? No thanks."

Brad stood up and shoved his chair into the table. "I'm out of here. Fuck you, Sami."

As he strode away, several thoughts formed in Samn's head. The only one that turned to words was, "It's Samn! Samn! My name's not fucking Sami!"

"Slut!" he bellowed as he vanished from sight.

Samn settled back into her chair and felt tears welling in her eyes. She folded her arms across her chest and tried to disappear. When the vanishing act didn't work, she called for the check. The waiter brought her a small black booklet and placed it on the table, avoiding her eyes. She and Brad had clearly made a scene.

She lifted the black booklet and peered inside.

"$189.44," she whispered, tears streaming down her face. "That fucking bastard."

Chapter 12

Mandy Goes to Nippletown

Samn arrived to a blur of blue and red lights at her apartment. Several police cars and an ambulance sat outside the building with lights on, sirens off. Samn's muscles tightened, and her breathing sped up at the sight, her mind immediately considering the worst case scenario.

"Hey! Samn!"

Mandy waved to her from across the crowded parking lot, her breath vaporizing in the chilled night air. She navigated the sea of people with a series of bumps, "I'm sorries," and "thank yous," and then found Samn's arms, hugging her tightly.

"How dare that bastard stick you with the check!" she said, brushing a stray strand of auburn hair behind her ear.

Samn had called Mandy as soon as she left the restaurant damn near $200 lighter than she had been when she entered. She told her everything, as friends do, and Mandy raged and joked Samn out of the sea of sadness.

Mandy, the ever-present life preserver.

"To hell with him," Samn said, barely believing the words as they escaped her mouth, for truthfully, she wanted nothing more than to wear oversized T-shirts, eat junk food and bitch about Brad all night. "What exactly happened here?" She motioned to the sirens and crowd of people who had gathered around the perimeter.

Some of the people she recognized; others she did not. At least one older couple lived in her building, but here they were at almost midnight huddled in bathrobes on the sidewalk.

"Not sure," Mandy said. "I left as soon as you called and just got here a little while ago."

"I'm going to find out."

"Samn, wait!" Mandy said, trotting after her.

Samn jogged over to the couple she recognized. "Excuse me. What happened here?"

The man, one hand tucked into his robe's pocket and the other held firmly around his wife's shoulders, looked at her with weary eyes. "Not 100% sure. Cops said something about a murder in the building."

"A murder?" Samn said.

"Did you fucking say murder?" Mandy said, joining Samn's side from where she had previously been eavesdropping. "Pardon my language," she quickly added, offering Mr. and Mrs. a wrinkle-nosed smile.

"That's what I said," the man said. "We don't even know who it is. Cops won't say anything yet. We don't even know if they caught the guy."

"Thank you," Samn said, and walked away arm-in-arm with Mandy.

"You don't think?" Mandy said, eyebrows raised.

"Sure, I do," Samn said. "I've seen what that thing can do. And we never caught it. It's definitely a possibility."

"Let's get out of here," Mandy said, massaging her breast absently.

"I need to get some clothes and stuff."

"Honey, I'll let you borrow anything you need. Let's go!"

"Brad doesn't deserve you," Mandy said, settling in beside Samn on her sofa and handing her a carton of chocolate ice cream and a spoon. "Not in the least."

"I think I'm starting to realize that," Samn said. She removed the ice cream lid and set it on the table in front of the couch. She pressed the spoon into the frosty surface and pried free a delicious scoop.

Mandy had delivered on all fronts so far: oversized T-shirts, check; junk food despite it being in the AM hours, check. Now, let the bitching about boys commence.

"I can't believe he jumped to cheating at the mere mention of another guy. I had a... problem. I had to get it checked out. It's not like I wanted Spider to feel me up!"

"Could have fooled me," Mandy said, smirking. She squeezed her breast, closed her eyes and moaned, "oh, Spider! Your fingers feel so good!"

"Shut the fuck up!" Samn said, but she couldn't help but smile which caused Mandy to burst into a fit of laughter. "It wasn't like that at all. That area had felt horrible lately and it was nice to not feel horrible for a second. That's all."

"Sure," Mandy said, rolling her eyes.

Samn popped the first bite of ice cream into her mouth and let it melt on her tongue.

"Good, huh?" Mandy said, taking a scoop from her own container.

Samn nodded and took another bite. As the ice cream soothed her dry throat, she noticed Mandy fidgeting with her breast again. She cast her a worried glance and said, "you ok?"

"Yeah," Mandy said. "I made the mistake of wearing my most uncomfortable bra today. It's a bit tight and the material made me itch a little." Samn's eyes widened. "Don't worry! It's not the nipple monster! Just a shitty bra. It's all good. Promise!"

"Have you talked to Spider today?"

"I haven't. Why? Want me to put in a good word for you?" She grinned.

"No! I'm just curious if he knows what happened to that thing."

"Last thing I heard him say about it is that it's so tiny we can't even see it. Judging from the scene at your apartment, it looks like that thing is someone else's problem now."

"That's awful," Samn said.

"I know!" Mandy said defensively. "I'm not saying I want other people to suffer. Just that I really DON'T want you to suffer."

Mandy rubbed her left nipple again without paying it much mind.

"I don't want you to suffer either," Samn said, eyeing Mandy's breast as though it were a poisonous snake.

"This is nothing a little time and lotion won't cure."

"If you say so," Samn said. "Besides, if that thing killed someone at my apartment, it can't be in your nipple too. One of the few tricks I haven't seen that thing play is being in two places at once."

"True!" Mandy said through a mouthful of strawberry ice cream. "You should have seen the inside of the building. There was blood everywhere."

"What? You were inside?"

"Just for a second," Mandy said. "When I got there and saw the cop cars, I rushed right inside to make sure you were ok. There wasn't anybody keeping people out at that point. There was blood all over the hallway. It freaked me out, so a cop walked me outside."

"Holy shit!" Samn said. She dropped her spoon into the ice cream container and placed it on the coffee table. "You were that close to the crime scene? Why didn't you tell me?"

"I didn't think it was that big of a deal," Mandy said. "I was only in there for a few minutes. And it's not like I went looking for the crime scene. It was just a few doors down from your apartment."

"Did you go inside the room where the murder happened?" Samn's eyes widened with fear and her voice trembled.

"No, the only blood I saw was what had spilled into the hall."

Samn drew her naked knees up under the oversized T-shirt and hugged them to her chest. She leaned back on the couch and pictured a grizzly crime scene just a few feet from where she sleeps, so bad that the blood escaped the room and leaked out into the hallway.

"It's too close," Samn said. "It has to be that thing. Someone is dead because of me!"

"No honey," Mandy said, drawing closer and placing a comforting hand on her forearm. "It isn't your fault. We did our best to capture that thing. How were we supposed to know cold would make it shrink?"

"Spider could have told us," Samn said, for the first time resenting the oddball fellow.

"True," Mandy said, "but how was he supposed to know we were going to refrigerate the little fucker?"

Mandy scratched her breast again.

"We should call Spider right now," Samn said, noticing. "What if that thing is in you now? You were in the building! It could have--"

"It didn't," Mandy said. "Itchy bra, remember? This isn't new. I should really throw the damn thing away, but bras are fucking expensive."

Samn's breathing and heart rate slowed. She drew in deep breaths through her nose and eased them out through her mouth.

"You had a traumatic experience to say the least," Mandy said, putting an arm around Samn. Samn recoiled when Mandy's breasts grazed her arm, but when she realized what she'd done she set an apologetic stare upon her friend. "It's all good." Mandy laughed it off. "Traumatic experience. I would call your behavior perfectly normal. Let's try to get some sleep."

"Do you want me to stay awake just in case..." Her voice trailed off, words lost, so she opted instead for nodding to Mandy's breasts.

"Not at all. You need your rest. When we wake up tomorrow morning and everything is perfectly fine, you'll feel a lot better."

For Samn, sleep proved elusive. She tossed and turned, tucked an arm beneath her head, rolled onto her back with legs crossed at the ankles, pulled blankets to her chin, kicked them off completely. Nothing helped. She couldn't help but keep an extra close eye on Mandy, who dozed off within seconds of her head hitting the pillow. Samn watched her until sleep finally came.

She woke to a tapping sound, like long painted nails on a wooden desk. She sat up in bed and rubbed sleep from her eyes, at first not realizing where she was. Surrounded by deep shadows cast by light streaming through the bedroom window, she saw only the curve of Mandy's hip next to her, body turned away from Samn, still resting peacefully.

"Mandy," Samn said, surveying the room with squinted eyes for the source of the tapping, which tapped at varying volumes and speeds, interrupted occasionally by a dry snapping sound. "Mandy, wake up!"

She leaned towards her sleeping friend to shake her awake, but ceased upon grasping a handful of soaked sheets. She lifted her hand from the shadows, extended it into the window's moonlight, and saw fingers streaked red. The sticky substance leaked down her hand and wrist.

"What the fuck? Mandy!"

She lunged forward and grasped Mandy by the shoulder.

"Wake up!"

She rolled Mandy onto her back and screamed, finally locating the source of the tapping sound.

Tap. Tap. Crack! Snap! Tap. Tap.

The papillasite sat upon Mandy's sternum just below the massacred remains of her breast, plowing through bone to reach her tender innards. Its teeth chomped on the gore that had once kept her friend alive. Tap. Tap. Tap. And occasionally, the monster would delve further into her guts, snapping bone when needed, pulling forth dripping entrails for its ongoing meal.

The moon mingled with streetlights and cast the papillasite's massive shadow onto the wall. Samn eased herself over the edge of the bed, shuddering, trying not to make much noise. She knelt beside the bed and cried into the side of the mattress, unable to shake the visage of Mandy's lifeless eyes.

How did I not wake up? she thought. This thing murdered my best friend, and I slept through it!

The thoughts permeated her panic, her fear, and solidified at the forefront of her mind: Mandy was gone. Her best friend, someone who had proved the moniker of "I'll do anything for you" 100 times over, someone who Samn would have died for, in her place, was dead.

Her trembling hands clenched into balled fists. Samn gritted her teeth and she glared at the monster with hateful eyes.

She crawled onto the bed careful not to make a sound. The papillasite seemed intent on its meal, unaware of its surroundings.

Samn lunged forward and wrapped a hand around its tiny arms and body, plunging her other hand inadvertently into Mandy's exposed and half-devoured guts. The creature shrieked and writhed. Samn felt its claws wiggling against her palm and fingers, but she squeezed tighter, ignoring the sting when one of them nicked the skin.

Samn kicked her legs over the side of the bed and rushed out of the bedroom fighting against the frantic papillasite. The thing screeched louder, its voice like the protest of a rusty hinge and unexpectedly loud for its size. It fought against the pressure of her closed hand and threatened to break free. Samn couldn't believe the strength it possessed, but then recalled Mandy's snapping ribs.

She closed another hand around it, careful to avoid its kicking clawed feet which dangled below her grasp. She traversed the familiar apartment in the dark with ease until she reached the kitchen.

She thrust the papillasite into the garbage disposal and covered it with a dirty plate. She flipped the disposal on and it whirred to life, grinding against the creature's tiny body. It screamed, hissed, and then growled as the disposal shuddered to a stop.

Silence.

Samn held the plate in place over the disposal, but it no longer lurched with a creature trying to break free. It sat still, an unwashed dish in the sink. Perfectly normal aside from the frantic, blood-soaked hands which held it down.

She lifted the plate and peeked beneath, but as soon as she presented a gap between sink and plate, a tiny, clawed hand shot forth and stabbed at her wrist.

Samn screamed and recoiled, but righted herself to make sure she didn't release the dish and let the thing escape. She slammed the plate against the creature's wrist several times until it retracted its hand back into the disposal.

With one hand still applying pressure against the plate, she flicked the disposal off and on, but nothing happened. She searched the room with wide eyes for a knife, a fork, something sharp, but before she could locate a weapon the papillasite burst through the plate, shattering the glass and mangling Samn's hand.

It skittered up her arm and leapt onto her chest. She smacked at it but withdrew when met with a flurry of jagged and chipped claws, no doubt a product of the failed attempt to feed the thing to the garbage disposal.

When presented with an opportunity, the creature shredded her shirt, exposing her breasts. It eyed the right breast for only a second but seemed confused by the surgical adhesive. Instead, it opted for the left, plunging its tiny body into the nipple, rending flesh as it burrowed into its new home.

No!" Samn screamed. "This has to be a dream! A fucking nightmare!"

But instead of waking, she toppled over, unconscious once more.

Chapter 13
ARACHNOPHOBIA

Samn woke to gloved hands and unfamiliar faces. Voices murmured all around her, but she discerned no meaningful dialogue, just the hum of a dozen or so voices.

She tried to sit up, but a gloved hand caught her shoulder and eased her back down.

"Easy ma'am," the man said, a cop about 30 years old. He wore a PD jacket and thin-rimmed glasses. Another man kneeled at her other side: a paramedic by the looks of his garb. "What happened here?"

"Let me make sure she's going to survive before the questioning begins," the paramedic said.

"What's going on?" Samn said, memory foggy and heart racing as if waking from a nightmare that blurred the lines between reality and dream. "Mandy! Where's Mandy?"

"Is that your roommate's name?" the cop said.

"She isn't my roommate. She's my friend. I was just staying over tonight. Is she...?"

"I'm afraid so, ma'am." The cop lowered his eyes. "Sit tight. Once the medics are done, I'd love to speak with you about what happened here tonight."

Samn nodded, tears in her eyes.

The cop stood and walked out of the kitchen toward the cloud of murmurs that most likely originated in the bedroom.

For a brief moment after waking, Samn thought it was all a dream. All of it. Amidst the panic and grief nestled a glimmer of hope that Mandy still lived and papillasites and monsters didn't exist, but the crowded apartment, her aching breast suggested otherwise.

"What exactly happened here?" the paramedic said, shining a light into her eyes.

"We were attacked," Samn said, blinking at the light. "I'm not sure what it was. I woke up and Mandy was..."

Her voice trailed off as memories of a gargantuan creature sitting atop Mandy's open sternum tearing dripping bits of her friend and piling them into its mouth flooded her mind.

Samn covered her mouth to stifle cries, but tears came anyway.

"Try to relax," the paramedic said. "The good news is you're going to be ok. A few bandages and so on."

I slept through Mandy's murder. If I had woken up, maybe I could have stopped that thing. What am I saying? I couldn't even stop that thing from getting back inside me.

Samn sat up causing a sheet to fall from her torso exposing her breasts. She glared down at them, from repaired right to freshly injured left. The oversized T-shirt Mandy had given her hung from her shoulders in tatters, the chest ripped open exposing several long scratches and one swollen nipple.

"Careful," the paramedic said, handing her the sheet and averting his eyes, though his gaze seemed to drift back to the swollen left nipple. "What exactly happened to your breasts?" he said. "Judging from the adhesive, this isn't the first time this has happened."

Samn took the sheet, but instead of covering up, she held it in her hands, gripping the fabric in clenched fists.

"That fucking monster!" she said, struggling for breath.

"It's ok, ma'am. You're safe now. The police are here. They're gonna catch him."

Can't catch that thing if it's dead, Samn thought. *I'll find a way to kill that little bastard.*

The paramedics brought Samn a clean, intact T-shirt from Mandy's closet: a navy blue with tall pink letters "P-I-N-K." Once her wounds were treated, Samn removed the tattered shirt in Mandy's bathroom and slipped the clean shirt over her head.

Despite Samn's insistence that she felt fine, the medic insisted she allow the ambulance to transport her to the local hospital for evaluation. She reluctantly agreed. The same cop assured her he would meet her there.

The ambulance jostled back and forth as the driver took turbulent turns and Samn felt that if she weren't strapped to the table she would have toppled off at several different points. The paramedic sat at her side and continually assured her everything would be alright.

After admissions and a few basic tests to check Samn's vitals, a nurse took her to a sterile room filled with false light. It reminded Samn of Dr. Sprake's office, so when the nurse asked her for her family doctor's name, she gave Sprake's name. At least he had been exposed to her story and didn't immediately dismiss it as crazy--not completely outright anyway. She cringed at the thought of sharing her outlandish tale with someone else.

Maybe this most recent evidence would lend her story credibility in Sprake's eyes.

The nurse informed her that she would inform Dr. Sprake of her condition and he would likely be in to see her tomorrow morning, and then she exited the room, leaving Samn alone with the beep and hiss of ER tech and an outdated sitcom she couldn't name playing on a tiny mounted TV.

Samn thumbed at her left nipple underneath the mandatory hospital gown. It didn't itch or hurt at the moment, but she knew that thing had to be in there. Just look at it! Puffy, swollen and red. Approximately twice the size of her right nipple.

Concern faded as exhaustion took over. Samn's foggy mind realized she had no way of telling how long she'd been unconscious, or even what day it was. How long had she been away from work? Did she even have a job anymore? These seemed like minor issues compared to her need for sleep.

As her eyes closed and the canned laughter on TV receded, someone opened the door and jolted her awake. Samn opened her eyes to see the policeman from Mandy's apartment. Another man--tall, with dark skin and a gray suit--followed him into the room. This man sported a well-groomed beard but no hair on his head.

"Hi Samantha," the policeman said. "Sorry to bother you. I promise this won't take long. My name is Officer Parente and this is Detective Moore. We just need to ask you a few questions and we'll get out of here and let you rest."

"Sure," Samn said, her mind racing horrendous outcomes should she decide to tell these men the truth. Would they lock her up? Blame her for Mandy's death? In a way, it was her fault. She sat upright in bed, wincing.

The officer closed the door to her room and stood beside it while the detective pulled a chair to Samn's bedside.

"I'm sorry to trouble you," Detective Moore said. "But the quicker we get started tracking down the person who did this, the better the chance we have of catching him."

"I understand," Samn said. "I'll do my best to help."

What the fuck am I going to say? Yes, detective, your suspect is about three to four inches tall--depending on how many tits he's recently snacked on, maybe bigger. It has razor sharp finger and toe nails, big yellow eyes, and sounds something like this "raaaauggghhheerrrhh!"

"Can you tell us who did this to you and your friend?" Detective Moore said, retrieving a small pad of paper and pen from his inner suit pocket.

Samn weighed her options, but in the interest of not taking too long to answer, she said, "I didn't get a great look at him. The room was super dark. When I woke up all I saw was that monster sitting on top of Mandy." She fought back genuine tears. "I tried to help, but he was too strong. At some point, I passed out after that thing attacked me."

"You're lucky to be alive." Detective Moore scrawled something into his notebook. "Are you sure the perpetrator is male?"

"Not 100% sure," Samn said, "but most likely. He was so strong."

"Did you get a look at hair color, eye color? Anything at all that may help identify this person?"

"I'm sorry. No."

Samn scratched at her cuticles, eyes downcast. Detective Moore scratched something else into his notebook. The sound reminded Samn of tiny toenails scratching hardwood floor.

"Around what time did you wake up?"

"I'm not entirely sure," Samn said. "Probably around 4 a. m."

More scratching. Samn's pulse raced, drummed in her veins, thumped at her temples. Sweat filled her palms. *Please make that scratching stop!* she thought.

"Is there anything else you'd like to share with us?" Detective Moore said, pausing his scratching pen to look her in the eyes.

"Not that I can think of."

"Well, get plenty of rest. If you think of anything tomorrow, please give me a call." He handed her a rectangular card containing his contact information.

"I will," she said, forcing a smile.

Detective Moore stood and left the room. Officer Parente started after him, but stopped and turned around, approached her bed.

"Almost forgot," he said, pulling Mandy's cell phone from his pocket. "You left this at the apartment. I thought you might want it."

"Actually, that's..." she almost said, "not mine," but thought better of it. Instead she said, "really thoughtful. Thank you."

Officer Parente handed her the phone and nodded, and then departed the room, closing the door behind him.

Samn tapped the screen and saw a photo wallpaper of her and Mandy, embracing each other at a Cradle of Filth concert. Samn wore a genuine, broad smile while Mandy grimaced, playfully showcasing her disdain for metal music. Samn remembered that day. Mandy tagged along despite not liking the band. She went for Samn because Samn's then-boyfriend had bailed on her. Fresh tears filled Samn's eyes, but she brushed them away and typed in Mandy's passcode.

She navigated to Mandy's contact list and scrolled until she saw "Spider." She opened the contact and tapped "call."

That little fucker seemed like it was afraid of Spider. If that was the case, she needed him more than any doctor right now.

"Hey Mandy, what's up?" Spider said on the other end of the phone.

"Spider, it's Samn. Remember me?"

"O'course," he said. "Everything ok?"

"No! That damned thing is back in my boob." She whispered into the phone for fear that someone would overhear. "And... and Mandy's dead."

"Dead? What the fuck happened?" His voice rang through the phone and filled the silent room, causing Samn to wince in fear, sure that someone had heard.

"That thing was inside her. It broke out and killed her."

"And now it's back in you?"

"Yes! I tried to kill it, but it was too strong. It nearly killed me too."

"Naw," Spider drawled. "It likes you. You're home."

"What do you mean?"

"It killed Mandy when it didn't need'er anymore. Lords of chaos rest her soul. But it doesn't just need you. It likes you. It wants to be inside of you."

Samn's thoughts involuntarily drifted to Brad, drawing similarities between him and the papillasite. *A little monster that always wants to be inside of me? Sounds about right.*

"So, discomfort's your only danger," he said, his voice shaking. "Now, of course, if you don't feed'im that all changes. Everything's gotta eat, ya know."

"So, I'm home until it needs an extra meal?"

"You got it," Spider said.

"What can we do? Can we kill it?"

"We can try. Where you at?"

"I'm in the hospital," Samn said.

"Hospital? What the fuck happened?"

"We have a lot to talk about," Samn said.

"Get some sleep," Spider said. "The thing just ate. It won't bother you too much 'til it needs to eat again. I'll come see you tomorrow."

Samn slept well.

She woke to a nurse's presence in the morning's early hours. The nurse checked a few things and provided breakfast. Samn ate very little, but then drifted back to sleep.

Before sleep took her, she thought, *I hope Spider gets here before Dr. Sprake.*

He did not.

The next time Samn woke, Dr. Sprake sat at her side, a laptop propped on his knees.

"Sorry to wake you," he said. "I know you've had a tough time lately. I just wanted to check in and see how you are doing."

Samn sat up in bed, used the automatic buttons on the side to raise the mattress to a sitting position.

"Not great," Samn said.

"These reports have certain," he hesitated, "commonalities with your previous injury. Can we talk about that?"

"I know you don't believe me, but I told you the truth in your office." Samn crossed her arms over her breasts, feeling overly exposed in the thin hospital gown.

"I'm not saying I don't believe you." He peered at her over the laptop screen. "I'm just saying that someone or something has hurt you multiple times and I can only help you if I have all the facts. Facts." He stressed the last word as if to say, "tell me the truth and I'll make it go away."

Samn said nothing. She didn't know what to say.

"Is there a man in your life?"

Samn shifted her gaze from a blank spot on the wall in front of her to Dr. Sprake's eyes. She nodded.

"Does he hurt you?"

"What? No!" Samn insisted. "Well, he's an asshole and pisses me off sometimes, but he never physically hurt me. He damn sure didn't do this!" She motioned to her breasts.

Dr. Sprake stared at his laptop screen, ran a hand over his chin and sighed.

"I'll order a mammogram," he said, his fingers flying over the keys of the laptop. "The nurses will come get you momentarily. I'll be back this afternoon to look over the results."

Samn nodded. Dr. Sprake cast her a sympathetic glance and left the room.

Samn's eyes drifted from low-volume sitcom to the digital display on Mandy's cellphone, and occasionally to the waning battery. She considered calling Spider again, but decided against it. He said he'd be here, so he'd be here.

Just before noon, a new nurse came by to check her vitals and bring lunch. The nurse wore blue scrubs, white shoes and a rainbow bandana tied around her head like a headband, holding her hair back out of her eyes. Samn cooperated, but didn't dare touch the questionable-looking food.

As she sat, spooning cold corn kernels around on her tray, a knock came at the door.

"'Scuse me, miss. Someone order an exterminator?" Spider peeked around the edge of the door. He wore no face paint, obviously, mangled jeans, black tank top and a denim jacket, sleeves rolled up. Several rings adorned his fingers and a spiked bracelet covered each wrist.

"What's with all the jewelry?" Samn said. "I almost didn't recognize you with the spider tattoos covered up." She motioned to the bracelets.

"Well, I didn't want the nurses to think I was weird or anything." He smiled a wounded smile and entered the room, taking the same seat Dr. Sprake had sat in earlier. "Did you have any...issues last night?"

"Slept like a baby," Samn said.

"Are you sure?" Spider's brow wrinkled, eyes drooping with worry. "I overheard a couple of nurses talking with the cops down the hall. Heard somethin' 'bout a patient that got killed last night. Sounded like our boy's M.O."

"What? It can't be." Samn said, covering her mouth with a trembling hand. "You said it wouldn't bother me since it just ate."

"I also told you when we first met, that I'm familiar with these damn things, but by no means an expert."

"Maybe if you were, Mandy would still be alive." The words escaped from behind her hand before she had a chance to stop them. "Spider, I'm sorry. I don't know why I said that."

"You said it, but we's both thinkin' it." His smile vanished, eyes drifted to the floor. "I've replayed that night over in my head 100 times. I should've left the shop, came home with you that night, took care of that thing myself."

Samn wanted to reassure him, make him feel better, but she knew all the words would ring hollow and false, so she opted to say nothing instead.

"Mandy's dead 'cause o' me," he said. "I'll help ye off this thing, then I'll get outta yer hair."

Samn nodded. "So, what do we do? I shoved that thing in a garbage disposal and it barely even scratched it."

"I must say I've never seen a papillasite with that much stayin' power. I brought this," he said, digging around in a fanny pack with a baphomet pentagram on it that she hadn't noticed until now.

He withdrew a tiny box, about five inches tall and three inches wide, adorned with black runes on each side.

"If we can't kill it we can keep it. So long as we can manage to get 'im in here."

He opened the door to the box and Samn peered inside, squinting to get a better look at the small interior, which was lined with spikes on all four sides.

"And he can't break out of that?" Samn said.

"Not a chance. I double and triple checked every single rune before I painted 'em on there. He won't be able to get outta there."

"So, how do we get it in there?"

"The little fella likes to come out while you're sleepin'. That's when he's fully awake and dangerous. We need to catch 'im while he's sleepin'."

"How do we do that?"

"You ain't gonna like it," Spider said, shaking his head.

"I don't like any of this. Just tell me so we can get this over with."

"We're gonna have to pull 'im outta there while you're awake. A tiny incision, some tweezers, he'll come right outta there."

Samn shuddered at the thought of nipple surgery, but it couldn't possibly be worse than when that thing bursts out.

"Ok, let's get it over with," she said, reaching behind her to untie the hospital gown.

"Hold yer horses," Spider said, holding up both hands. "Don't ye want me to try and find something to numb it with. We are in a hospital after all."

"I'm not worried about the pain. It can't be worse than when he breaks out on his own." Samn realized she was not referring to the thing as "he," just like Spider.

"Fair enough." He rose from the chair, walked to the door and closed it, locked it. He crept to the nurse's station, an awkward tip-toed gate, near a mockery of actual sneakiness, opened the cabinet and rummaged around. Moments later, he pulled forth a bottle of rubbing alcohol, gauze and a few silver instruments. He tore free some paper towels and spread them out on the counter, and then sorted the instruments upon it.

Samn untied the hospital gown and pulled it to the side, exposing her left breast. She looked down at the nipple, still puffy and somewhat discolored, but not the mangled mess it had been after the little creep's last outbreak.

That thing was huge the last time it crawled inside me, she thought. *If it came out to play last night, wouldn't I be in way worse shape than this?*

She considered saying something to Spider, but decided against it. She reclined the bed to a more horizontal position and lay back, hands folded on stomach, eyes fixed on ceiling.

"Ready," she said.

Spider pulled on a pair of latex gloves, poured alcohol on a piece of gauze and used it to wipe down Samn's breast. She winced at the touch of the cool liquid and Spider's sterile latex fingers. Spider leaned close and examined the breast, poking the tissue with two fingers until he said, "got ya."

Holding two fingers on Samn's breast, he stretched to the counter and retrieved a scalpel and tweezers.

"You sure you're ready?" he said. "This ain't gonna feel good."

Samn nodded, eyes still fixed on the ceiling.

Spider knelt over her and eased the scalpel into the tender flesh of her areola where his fingers had been. Samn winced, but stifled a cry. Blood streamed down her breast and pooled at her side. Samn bit her lip to keep from screaming. The pain wasn't quite as bad as when the papillasite birthed itself, but at least then she had the freedom to scream as much as she liked.

Enduring this was one thing; enduring it quietly was something else.

"There we go," Spider said, again keeping two fingers on her breast while placing the scalpel back on the counter and retrieving fresh gauze. "How we doin'?"

"I'm ok," Samn said through gritted teeth. "Just get this thing out of me."

Spider spread the wound just far enough to see the sleeping creature. It nestled inside the breast in a cocoon of glandular tissue, knees tucked to chest, tiny arms hugging them.

"This thing looks to be about four inches tall," he said. "Ain't no way he busted outta here last night without you knowin'. Somethin' else must've killed that other person."

"Comforting," Samn said, unsure if she actually meant it or not.

"Just hold real still and I'll have 'im outta there in no time."

He inserted the tweezers into the wound, pushing the incision further open causing fresh blood to spurt forth. Samn gasped and a painful moan escaped her pursed lips. She covered her mouth with her hand.

Using the tweezers, he grasped the sleeping creature around the waist and tugged. Sharp pain spread through Samn's breast, originating at the point of the tweezers. The creature resisted, using its tiny hands to latch onto the surrounding tissue. Samn's body lurched as she struggled to stop her cries.

Her breast tissue popped. Samn felt it, heard it. Felt fresh, warm blood trickling down her skin. Samn chanced a look at the breast in time to see the tiny creature emerge from her blood-spattered flesh at the tip of the tweezers, its eyes closed, limbs limp, sleeping peacefully.

Spider held the creature in front of his face just as the eyes opened. It writhed on the tip of the tweezers, emitted a screech, flailed its arms and legs, a flurry of sharp claws. Spider didn't flinch, instead tightened his grip.

"Look at me, you little shit," he said, snarling into the thing's face.

The papillasite fixed its eyes on Spider and once again fell limp, hanging from the tweezers like the world's largest blackhead. Blood ran down its body and dotted the white tile floor. The creature's shrieks became whimpers.

"You fucked with yer last titty, my friend," Spider said, and then dropped the docile creature into the rune box.

Chapter 14

And the Walls Ran Red with Blood

Spider held the rune box in both hands, eyeing it as if expecting it to break open any second. He retrieved a ribbon from his jeans pocket and set it and the box on the counter. From his other pocket, he produced a small bottle of black nail polish, proceeding to paint similar runes on the ribbon. When finished, he gently blew the polish dry and stepped back to admire his handy work.

"This ought to hold 'im," he said, tying the ribbon around the box, the ends coming together in a delicate bow in front of the door. "Just don't take that ribbon off, and definitely don't open that door."

He pulled another bottle from somewhere, as if in addition to occultist, the man was also a magician with bottomless pockets, and spritzed the box with a pleasant smelling liquid.

"What's that for?" Samn said.

"Just perfume. Friend o' mine said they like the smell o' cherry blossom. This one has a little somethin' extra in it. Just spray 'im once a day. Sates his thirst. Makes 'im nice and docile."

He handed Samn the bottle.

"And if I run out? I'm guessing the kind you can buy at Bath and Body doesn't have the little something extra?"

"I stock it at my shop," he said. "First one's on the house. Figure I didn't do too good at dealin' with this thing. Next bottle'll be $19.99. Gotta make a livin', ya know?"

Samn nodded.

"Let's get you cleaned up, patched up 'fore the docs come in and get their underclothes all wadded up."

Spider knew his way around a medical setting, expertly disinfecting and mending the incision. Samn found herself gazing at him, his shaved head brimming with stubble outlining his receding hairline, the rows of silver rings piercing his ears, his soft lips and dark puppy dog eyes, tender but also possessing something fierce. She tug-of-warred with lust and hate. Mandy had faith in this man and now she's dead, but deep down Samn knows Spider never meant her harm.

"There ye go," he said. "I'll...be going now." He backed away from her. "Again, I'm truly sorry 'bout Mandy."

Just as he reached the door, unlocked it and turned the knob, Samn said, "wait."

His eyes met hers, pleading for forgiveness.

"Thank you," she said. A cyclone churned in her mind, and an array of emotions she didn't quite understand, didn't want to understand. She wanted someone, Mandy perhaps, to calm the cyclone, tame it, pull out resentment, anger, hate and squash them under heel, leaving behind only curiosity, tenderness, lust. Sympathy.

"Don't beat yourself up about Mandy." She paused, hesitated, felt the words tumble past reluctant lips. "It wasn't your fault." She forced herself to meet his eyes.

Spider exhaled a long breath, as if he'd been holding it for quite some time.

"I 'ppreciate that," he said, smiling. "Ye got my number if ye need me."

He opened the door and exited the room, eyes lingering on Samn until he disappeared.

Samn winced as she placed her breast on the mammogram machine, a technician standing by to ensure optimal placement. Never before had she felt more like a piece of meat presented on a platter. It didn't help that the platter was bitterly cold to the underside of her boob.

"Stand perfectly still," the technician said, a woman of about forty years with auburn hair and dark eyes. "Compression may be uncomfortable, but it will only take about thirty seconds."

The machine pressed, pressing cold plate into cold plate, squashing her boob flat in the process. Samn bit her lip.

Uncomfortable, my ass! This hurts!

The pressure release and her boob slowly reclaimed its original form. Samn stepped away and closed her gown, massaging the tender area and making sure that the incision site didn't pop open.

"Ok, all done," the technician said. "Dr. Sprake only ordered a mammogram of the left breast, so you can return to your room. The doctor will be in to discuss the results with you soon."

Samn exited the room and walked down the hallway with arms crossed over her chest. She followed signs and arrows until she arrived back at the patient rooms.

A cop in a navy blue jacket, badge proudly displayed over the breast pocket, stood behind the nurse's station conversing with a distraught nurse. Samn approached the station, leaned in and whispered, "excuse me. Is something wrong?"

She remembered what Spider had said about the dead patient, but she needed to hear it from someone else to make it real--not for lack of trust in Spider, but because tragedies are easily ignored if second hand in nature.

The nurse buried her face in her hands and the policeman approached the counter at the front of the nurse's station.

"Please go back to your room, ma'am," he said.

Samn relaxed, realizing this was not the same cop from Mandy's apartment.

"Sure," Samn said, "but if something is going on, don't I have a right to know? We all put our lives in this hospital's hands." Her voice rose, echoing throughout the empty halls.

"Please keep your voice down," the cop said. "I don't want to cause mass panic."

"I'll keep it down," Samn said, "but I'm not going back to my room until you tell me what's up. I want to feel safe. I'm sure the other patients do too!"

He leaned closer, propping his elbows on the counter. "There's been another death on this floor," he whispered.

Samn played dumb.

"It's a hospital," she said. "People die here all the time. What brings the cops in?"

He sighed, tensed his posture. "We have reason to suspect foul play."

"Foul play? Like murder?"

The policeman nodded reluctantly. "That's why I prefer patients stay safely in their room until we know more."

"I understand," Samn said. "Apologies, officer."

Samn searched every shadow, every nook in the hallway, for tiny yellow eyes, a glint of light reflecting off tiny claws and teeth, any sign of movement. She saw nothing out of the ordinary.

She returned to her room and opened the door.

"Holy shit! No!" she said, clasping one hand firmly over her left breast, the other over her gaping mouth.

The rune box lay on its side bathed in the dim glow of silent sitcoms, its ribbon slashed in two, its door open.

Keeping one hand clasped over her boobs, she cautiously crept to the bed and retrieved Mandy's cell, sifted through the contacts and tapped on "Spider."

The phone rang as she searched the deep shadows of the room, feeling the thing's creepy ass eyes on her, waiting for the perfect opportunity to thrust itself back inside her nipple.

"Hello," Spider said.

"That thing escaped the box!"

"What? How the fuck?"

"I don't know," Samn said. "I left the room for some tests and when I came back the ribbon was cut and the door was open. That thing is not inside! What do I do?"

"First of all, that thing didn't bust outta there. He had help. Somebody or something cut that ribbon and let the little son of a bitch out."

"What? Who?"

"Get outta that room," Spider said. "Matter o' fact, get outta the hospital if you can. I got a bad feelin' 'bout this. I can be there in twenty minutes. I'll meet you out front."

Samn breathed panicked breaths into the phone. "Do you think it will come after me again?" She sobbed despite best efforts not to.

"Not it," Spider said. "Them. Think about it. Murder on your floor. Something cut the ribbon and opened the box. There has to at least be one more on that floor. That's why you need to get outta there. Right now! I'm on my way."

Spider hung up and Samn felt alone, even though he had just been a voice on the phone. She listened for the clatter of claws on tile, but heard nothing. Searched the shadows for glowing eyes, but saw nothing.

She tossed the phone onto the bed and ran to the closet where Spider had stored the clothes he bought for her. She pulled on the jeans and they mostly fit--perhaps, a little baggy. She shed the gown and lifted the bra from the clothes hanger where Spider had awkwardly hung it.

Definitely not a titty expert, she thought.

The chilled air birthed gooseflesh across her chest, hardened her nipples. She removed the tags from the bra and checked the size: 36C. A perfect fit.

Good hand-eye coordination though. A few squeezes and he knows my perfect bra size.

She slid the bra over her arms and had it halfway fastened when she caught sight of the black nail polish. Spider had left it on the bedside table. Her eyes drifted from nail polish to rune box to bra.

If the runes will keep the creature in, maybe if I paint them backwards it'll keep it out too.

She pulled the bra back off and spread it on the bed. She snatched the nail polish from the table and uncapped it. Analyzing the runes carefully, she painted them backward in a circular pattern around each bra cup, and then blew it gently so the polish would dry faster.

She stepped back and compared the runes. If not a perfect match, it was damn close. She grinned and slid the bra back on, feeling more secure against the threat of evil titty parasites, as if the bra were armor, not a cheap Wal-mart bra.

She reached for the last piece of Spider's impromptu ensemble: a gray hooded sweatshirt. She flipped it around in her hands and pulled it over her head, pushing arms through as needed. The hoodie hung from her frame like a bedsheet on a ghost, reaching damn near to her knees.

You were so close, Spider. So close.

"Shit!" A jolt of pain struck her in the chest, not in the boob, but along her breast bone, followed by an otherworldly shriek. Her shirt jutted this way and that as something fought to break free, something whose biggest fear was beautiful breasts.

Samn screamed and tugged at the shirt, trying to pull it over her head. When the shirt came free, familiar yellow eyes bored into her.

The papillasite pushed its claws into the flesh peaking above her bra and pushed away from her as if it had just stepped on hot coals. It landed on the mattress and stared at her in disbelief, its flesh sizzling. Samn shifted her eyes from it to the rune bra and back to the creature.

"Yeah, fucker! Stay the hell off of me!"

The creature's screams turned to low rumbles, a hellish growl coming straight from its guts. It propped itself up and poised to strike. Samn backed away, but not quickly enough. The creature lunged at her and latched itself to her shoulder, clawing and biting at the exposed flesh. Blood gushed from fresh wounds, ran down her arm. She screamed and swatted at the creature, but it paid her no mind.

The creature raked, ripped and tore at her flesh, mangled the skin and the meat beneath. It sank its teeth into the gore and tore free a chunk.

Samn screamed, cried, fell to the floor as the creature worked its way down her arm. She crawled through a pool of her blood, slippery and still warm, slowly pulling herself towards the cabinet.

She tried to ignore the pain as fresh scratches and bites peppered her arm. She opened the cabinet door and flailed about inside, looking for anything that may free her of the creature.

Samn grabbed a collection of silver instruments as the creature perched upon her shoulder, ceasing its biting for a moment. It brought its claws down across her clavicle, slashing the skin and severing the bra strap. The left cup remained in place, but drooped from her chest without the shoulder strap's support.

"No you don't!" Samn said, pulling a scalpel from the collection of silver instruments. She thrust the blade into the creature's sternum just as it crossed her back and mounted her right shoulder, presumably to slash the second strap.

The creature gasped, shrieked, its wound spewing black, hot liquid onto Samn's shoulder and chest. It clutched the scalpel in its hand and toppled backwards off of Samn's shoulder.

Samn crawled away from the creature as it struggled to remove the scalpel from its flesh. She used the door handle to pull herself to her feet, and then she turned the handle and stumbled out into the hallway, oblivious to her nakedness.

"Help!" she screamed. "Please help me!"

She approached the nurse's station as fast as her weary legs would allow, lurching the last few feet to grab the counter before she tumbled to the floor.

"Please help," she gasped, clutching her left shoulder. "There's a monster in my..."

She looked up and saw the same middle-aged nurse, her vacant eyes staring at the ceiling as a large papillasite feasted on her throat. Another creature had torn her shirt open and had bored into her stomach. It peered out from a baseball-sized hole in the woman's flesh, its teeth dripping with its latest meal. Both creatures were larger than her creature: throat guy standing at about six inches, and though it was hard to tell stomach guy's size, his dime-sized eyes suggested he was even larger than the other.

Samn backed away from the gore hoping the creature's hadn't spotted her, or at the very least, were more engaged with their existing prey than with the temptation of a new quarry.

A scream echoed out of the hallway, and seconds later all the lights went out. Samn flailed about in the pitch black, imagining approaching papillasites reaching for her legs. Seconds later, emergency backup lights kicked on offering meager illumination at regular intervals up and down the hallways. Samn jolted, hearing one of the nurse's bones snap. She made sure both papillasites were still feasting and crept down the hallway toward a glowing "exit" sign.

The screams turned to moans, to gurgling whimpers, and then silence.

The silence stopped Samn's shuffling footsteps. She stood still, held her breath, waited for more screams, shrieks. Instead, the sounds of flesh tearing from bone, like footsteps squelching through thick mud.

Samn rushed to the source of the sounds and found the door to the room open. A woman lay in bed, a papillasite perched on her chest, her sternum cracked open, split from clavicle to navel. The creature, standing at about seven inches tall, pulled handful after handful of gooey innards from the cavity and stuffed them greedily into its mouth.

Samn screamed, but cupped a trembling hand over her mouth when the creature peered up from its meal, its jaws still dripping with gore. It leapt from the woman's chest and clattered across the floor. Samn backed away and slammed the door closed just in time to block the monster's path.

She stumbled away from the room and further into the darkened hallway. She passed several closed doors and a few opened ones, careful not to look inside or make too much noise as she passed for fear that more papillasites lurked within. The hospital halls stood empty and dark, but even with limited visibility, she remembered where the elevators were.

Elevators? That's suicide, she thought. *Stair well.*

Samn hobbled down the hall, desperately trying to run. The walls spun around her. Floor became ceiling, ceiling floor. She squeezed her eyes together and then stretched them open. The blurry emergency lights glared down at her, blocking much needed vision. Still, she saw the general layout of the floor, and she clenched fists and squinted, forcing it further into focus.

A shriek filled the hallway, and then another. Soon a chorus of otherworldly bellows chased her down the hall, each one sounding closer than the last.

Samn turned and just barely discerned an army of creatures pattering towards her, though she struggled to tell which ones were real and which were the product of her blurry, duplicative vision.

The creatures' eyes joined the emergency lights--simple pin pricks in the distance--to further obscure Samn's sight. She pushed on, urging her legs to work harder.

How did they find me? I'm positive they weren't following me!

This thought drew awareness to the fresh blood seeping from between Samn's panicked fingers as they clutched her wounded arm. The blood drew Samn's gaze to the floor and to the long trail of dark blood blotting the hospital tiles.

Blood crumbs, Samn thought, her mind deliriously conjuring a fairy tale and blending it with reality.

She saw the elevator--suicide--at the end of the hall, an indiscernible red light shining above it that Samn was certain read EXIT. She crashed into the elevator door, her outstretched hand smashing the down button, the wall holding her spaghetti legs perpendicular to the floor.

I'd never make it down the stairs like this, she thought. *Suicide it is.*

"Come on!" she shouted, repeatedly slamming her thumb into the down button.

The jagged toenails of an unknown number of papillasites thrummed against the hospital tile, their tiny legs a blur. The sound reminded Samn of an impatient teacher's fingertips rhythmically pattering against a desktop, as if to say, "go on. What do you have to say for yourself?"

Samn's knees buckled as more blood poured from her wounds and pooled at her feet. The approaching papillasites shrieked as they drew closer, their voices, those nails echoed inside Samn's head.

Just as Samn hit her knees, the elevator door dinged open. She crawled inside on hands and knees and stretched upward to repeatedly smash the lowest button. She peered out the doors, which had yet to move despite her best efforts. The creatures drifted in and out of focus, their tiny feet leaving blood trails down the hall.

They're almost here! I'm going to die.

Her button smashing became button tapping and then she gave up, allowing herself to sit back against the cool reflective wall of the elevator. Their voices filled the tiny space just as the elevator doors hummed to life, closing on her impatient teachers as their hungry, eager claws reached out to her.

Her stomach lurched as the elevator descended.

Thank god for people who can't walk, Samn thought, gazing up at the bright overhead lights with tired eyes. Hospitals prioritize elevators when the power's out.

She laughed. Looks like suicide saved her life. For now.

The elevator door dinged open and Samn jerked awake.

I fell asleep? she thought incredulously. *How the fuck does someone fall asleep during a monster invasion?*

She wasn't sure, but she'd done it.

Blood had pooled around her while unconscious. She crawled toward the door and felt it soak the knees and shins of her pants. She caught a glimpse of her reflexion in the reflective elevator wall: pale as fuck, dark circles under eyes.

I look like a fucking corpse, she thought. Metal.

She chose to avoid looking directly at her lacerated arm and shoulder.

She crawled out of the elevator door and used a nearby water fountain to pull herself to her feet. Her legs shook as they struggled to support her weight.

She surveyed the area, searching every recess for lurking danger. She saw no papillasites, but they could have rampaged through here. The first floor of the hospital looked like a cross between an artsy monochromatic painting and a blood spatter analysis room.

Blood and chunks of flesh coated the walls in wide splotches and trailed along the floor. Bodies lined the floor in tattered heaps of meat and exposed bone.

Her vision lost focus again as if to protect her from the grizzly sight.

"Samn!" a familiar voice called from the distant entrance.

Footsteps approached, and then strong arms lifted her up.

"Spider?" she said.

"Yeah, it's me, darlin'." He supported her beneath her arms with freezing hands, and then turned to allow her to lean on him.

"Let's get the hell out of here," she said weakly.

They hobbled toward the sliding doors, which repeatedly opened and closed, obstructed by a corpse's legs, and frigid winter air collided with Samn's exposed skin. Spider removed his denim jacket and wrapped it around her shoulders.

"I'm parked just over here," he said, motioning to an old Camaro, matte gray with dimpled primer.

Spider led her to the passenger's side door and opened it. Samn collapsed into the seat and hugged the denim jacket around her body. The garment engulfed her petite frame. He hurried around the car, patting the hood as if for encouragement, and then leaped into the drivers' seat.

He turned the key and the engine sputtered to life, a growling rumble that shook the car's interior. Samn examined their surroundings with wide eyes, lingering longer on the exit.

No sign of papillasites.

She slumped back into the seat and exhaled as if she'd been holding her breath since she left her hospital room. She pulled the jacket off her injured shoulder. Now that she wasn't alone, she easily mustered the courage to examine the wound thoroughly.

"Damn!" Spider said, splitting his attention between the asphalt and Samn. "That thing did a number on you."

"Things," Samn said, wincing.

"I figured they's another one. At least. How many'd ye see?"

Samn closed her eyes, forcing the grizzly images to replay in her head. "At least four," she said. "But there must've been more! The first floor was a bloodbath!"

She lowered her head and sobbed in the shadows.

"Easy," Spider said. "You're safe now. Let's get back to my place and we'll fix you up."

Chapter 15

ARACHNOPHILIAC

"That is damn nice," Spider said, eyeing Samn's chest, her C cups visible beneath his denim jacket.

"Excuse me?" Samn said, shrugging off sleep. She'd fallen asleep in the car–or passed out, it was hard to tell–but Spider was able to jostle her awake once they arrived at his home, an antiquated A-frame on the historic side of town. The house surprised Samn with its size and stateliness, yet its gray paint, black trim and plum-colored door all reassured her that a Spider dwelled here.

"The runes," Spider said. "You do them?"

"Oh," Samn said, looking down at the bra's remains, each cup featuring a circle of runes around the nipples beneath. "Yeah, I just figured that if those symbols can keep it in the box, maybe they can keep it out of me."

"Did it work?"

"It must have. The damned thing nearly killed me trying to remove the bra. Been a while since I've had a date like that."

Spider chuckled. "Follow me. Bathroom's this way. Let's get a bandage on that damage."

She followed him through the house, dimly lit and void of sound, save for the clack of their footfalls on the hardwood floor. He opened a door across from the staircase and flipped on the light before entering. The overhead bulb filled the room with blinding white light.

"Have a seat," Spider said, patting the closed toilet lid.

Samn sat down and removed the denim jacket, wincing when the fabric tugged at the raw wounds on her shoulder and arm. Spider rummaged around in the cabinet, finding ointment and gauze. He washed his hands and applied soap and water to a washcloth.

"Be honest," Samn said, as Spider cleaned the wounds with the washcloth. "Are you a doctor on the side?"

"Not quite," Spider said. "Med school drop out." He kept his attention focused on his task, careful not to cause Samn any unnecessary pain.

"Why'd you drop out?" Samn winced as the cloth grazed a deep cut.

"My heart was in the occult," he said, winking. "More money in it too."

"You're saying you make more money as an occultist than you would have as a doctor?"

Spider laughed and placed the washcloth on top of the sink. The wounds looked less serious without all the dried blood: a series of lacerations, a few of which were deeper than the others.

"Way I see it, I'm still helpin' people, and doin' what I love. Money's mostly tied up in the business, so I'll not be takin' any swanky vacations any time soon. Still, it's worth it. Dress the way I want. Live the way I want. Answer to myself. More my style."

"I get it," Samn said. "I think that's what everybody wants at the end of the day. Few people actually get it, so congrats."

"Thank ye," he said. "Wish my parents felt that way."

He applied the ointment to the cuts. The cream cooled the wounds providing a degree of relief. Once finished, he turned back to the cabinet.

"I think one o' them is gonna need stitches."

"Stitches?" Samn said. "Can't we just glue it like we did this?" She motioned to her breast.

"Cut's too jagged, too deep. That little feller got ye good."

"You've done this before, though. Right?"

He eyed her and smirked. "Indeed."

"You own this house?" Samn said, eyes focused on the ceiling so that she didn't accidentally glimpse the needle penetrating her skin.

"I do," Spider said. "I'd love to tell ye I earned it, but it was willed to me. Prob'ly one of the reasons my folks don't talk to me no more."

Samn winced, bit her lip.

"Sorry," he said. "Almost done."

Once finished, he placed everything back in the cabinet and exited the room. Samn chanced a look at her arm, expecting it to be a mangled mess, but instead it was bandaged neatly.

"I ain't got no bras," Spider said, "but I got plenty o' T-shirts."

He tossed her a faded black garment. Samn unfolded it and held it up. A familiar nude ballerina, arms extended above head, throat cut, adorned the shirt beneath tall white letters: SUSPIRIA.

"You an Argento fan?" Samn said, smiling.

"Anybody who's anybody is," he said. "You dig 'im?"

"What kind of question is that?" Samn said. "Of course! I live and breathe horror movies. But the Italian stuff just hits different, you know?"

"That I do," Spider said.

Samn slid the shirt over her head. It was clearly a size too big and hung on her frame more like an oversized night shirt. Still, it felt good to be back in clothing that didn't make her want to puke.

"You hungry?" Spider said.

"Starved!"

"Kitchen's this way. I'll whip us somethin' up."

Spider heated up some canned spaghetti and they ate in silence. Samn acknowledged the irony of eating canned pasta in such a grandiose house, but smiled, crediting irony to inheritance, which had a way of mingling past values with current.

Irony or not, Samn was just thankful to have something other than hospital food.

To her surprise, Spider washed their plates as soon as they finished eating and placed them back in a cabinet.

"How 'bout a little music?" Spider said, his voice filling the otherwise silent house.

"Sure. That seems like such a normal thing to do, and I could go for a little normal."

She followed him through the house, eyeing extravagant decor as they walked: walnut bookshelves lined with occult books and Chuck Palahniuk novels, a towering grandfather clock that didn't seem to work, and a corner desk with an actual typewriter sitting atop. Everything was dusted and polished.

"Vinyl collection's right over here."

Spider stooped next to a large record player, which looked more like a TV stand. It featured a turntable on top, speakers on the sides, and convenient storage space directly in the middle. He opened the doors to the storage space and combed through the records, which all stood up straight, packed from side to side.

Samn knelt next to him and squinted to see the tiny print on the records' spines. She wasn't sure what to expect. Spider's look screamed metal, but the twang in his voice suggested country.

Asagraum. Cannibal Corpse. Emperor. Fulci!

Samn stared at him in disbelief. She had actually met another human with similar taste in music. She pulled Fulci's Tropical Sun from the shelf, but in doing so, stopped to notice that all albums were alphabetized by artist name, and just a few vinyls to the left, Dolly Parton had taken up residence between Deicide and Emperor.

"Hmm, Cannibal Corpse or Dolly Parton. I can't decide." Samn said mockingly.

Spider chuckled. "Don't be hatin' on Dolly, now. She's as metal as they come."

"Dolly? Metal?" Samn snickered.

"She gives a shit about people, ya know. Does everything in the world to help folks out. That's metal as fuck in my book."

"No argument from me," Samn said. "But let's go with Fulci."

"Fair enough," Spider said, taking the record from its slip and placing it on the turntable.

The needle grazed the surface and static filled the room followed by the electronic hum of the opening track. Spider turned the volume down a bit.

"Don't want to wake the neighbors," he said, smiling.

Samn closed her eyes and experienced healing as only her favorite bands could provide—not healing of the body, but healing of the spirit. And her spirit, along with her tits, had been through hell lately. She sat flat on the floor and leaned back against the record cabinet. Even at a lower than usual volume, Fulci's erratic bass drum massaged her back.

"Accordin' to my peers, those runes'll keep those things at bay."

Samn opened her eyes. "Peers? Occultists have peers?"

"Doesn't everybody?" Spider rubbed a hand over his stubbled scalp. "One lady, name o' Maureen but everybody in the business calls her Shadowcub on account o' her dad bein' called Shadowwolf, said those critters can't cross any surface with these runes on it. She's the first person to ever tell me 'bout these papillasites. Just wish she'd've told me 'bout the runes sooner. Mandy may still be alive."

"How well did you know her? Mandy, I mean."

"Not super well, but she was a customer, ya know. Never had any real problems I could help her with, just a healthy curiosity. She was a good person." Sorrow consumed his face and a tear spilled from his eye.

"She was, indeed," Samn said. She wiped the tear from his cheek and he flinched at her hand's touch. "I'm sorry I blamed you. I was just scared and pissed. Too many emotions, not enough sense."

Spider looked at her, eyes shining, mouth slightly open.

"Everybody let's emotion get the better of 'em sometimes. Just look at me. I'm a blubberin' mess. But there was some truth in what you said. If I'd been better prepared, she prob'ly wouldn't've died."

"Will you learn from that mistake?"

The question drew Spider's full attention to her. His drifting eyes snapped back to her as if she'd stabbed him.

"O' course I will," he said, voice wavering. "Already have. That's why I called Shadowcub and really pressed her for info. That's how I learned about the runes."

Samn stared up at the ceiling high above her, pictured the runes in her mind, envisioned various places to paint them.

"Does it matter what they're painted with?"

"If it does, S.C. never told me about it. I just used old nail polish. Nothin' special about it."

"I have an idea," Samn said, smiling, feeling the music pulsing against her back, bobbing her head to the death metal battery. "Can you round up any weapons you own and something to paint with?"

Spider grinned. "I think I know where you're goin' with this. I'm not sure the runes can be used as a weapon though."

"I'm fairly certain they can be," Samn said. "When I slid my shirt on after painting the runes on my bra, the creature was inside the shirt. It screamed like it was in pain. And then I stabbed it with a scalpel. That suggests the runes at least weakened it because I put the fucker in a garbage disposal at Mandy's and all it did was chip its nails."

"I'll fetch some weapons then," Spider said, standing and hurrying off through the large house. "Sit tight."

Samn closed her eyes again and allowed Fulci's guttural screams to envelop her. The perfect music to listen to as you create paranormal weaponry to take on an army of nipple parasites.

She heard Spider's sock feet pattering against the floor, growing louder as he returned to the room.

"This enough?" he said, holding an armful of steel and a tiny bottle of nail polish.

He dropped to his knees and eased the weaponry to the floor. The pile contained two lock-back pocket knives, one decorative dagger, a pair of brass knuckles, several pieces of finger armor—some people call these rings, but those people are fucking insane considering you could easily slit someone's throat with them—a black handgun and an unopened package of bullets. He set the nail polish next to the weapons.

"Let's get to paintin'," he said.

Samn uncapped the nail polish, picked up one of the lock-back pocket knives and opened its blade. Approximately three inches long, the steel blade gleamed even in the dim lighting. Samn unfastened her bra and slid her arms out, retrieving the undergarment from beneath her shirt like an underwear magician. She laid it down next to the knife for reference and started painting. Moments later, tiny black runes adorned the blade, three on each side.

"Now, that's a thing o' beauty," Spider said. "I hope you're right. That this'll hurt 'em I mean."

"We'll never know if we don't try," Samn said, retrieving the next knife and opening its blade.

She and Spider continued to paint runes until every sharp object contained at least six. Spider lifted the decorative dagger by its black, jeweled hilt and waved it around like a child with the best stick in the forest.

"Pretty damned neat," he said.

Samn cracked open the package of bullets and retrieved one.

"This is fucking small," she said. "Do we know exactly how many runes need to be there to get rid of the creatures?"

"Shadowcub just told me to paint the ribbon with these six runes." He gestured to the knife blade. "She never said to put them in any certain order or anything. If I had to guess, all six need to be there for max effect, but one'd prob'ly still make a dent."

"I don't think..." Samn began, but Spider cut her off.

"Don't worry," he said. "I learned from my mistake. I'll call Shadowcub now and ask some questions."

He pulled out his cellphone, navigated the contact list and tapped "Shadowcub."

Samn heard the beginning of their conversation as Spider walked out of the room. Moments later, he paced back into the room, listening intently, cellphone pushed to his ear.

"Yeah," he said. "Which one? I don't wanna fuck this up." He winked at Samn and then paced back out of the room.

Without her bra, Samn felt naked. It wasn't that her nipples poked through the black fabric–Spider had seen her tits almost more than Brad at this point–but without the runes to protect her, her tits were fair game if any of those monsters had followed them from the hospital.

Or maybe there's more! Samn thought, eyes widening in fear. *What if the whole world is infested and we never knew it?*

"Alright. I 'ppreciate ye, S.C.," Spider said, wandering back into the room. He tapped the red button to end the call and slid his phone back into his pocket.

"What'd she say?" Samn said, impatiently.

"She said one rune won't kill 'em, but it'd sure hurt like hell." He smiled, and Samn found herself grinning back. "She also said that if we're just gonna put one rune on a bullet, use this one."

He pointed to a rune with a fluid line on the left and a series of indentions connected to the right.

"That's the one that'll make those little fuckers feel like a cat's got ahold o' their balls."

"I like the sound of that," Samn said, removing her shirt and lifting her bra. She had grown tired of feeling unprotected.

Spider's smile faded and he covered his eyes and turned around. "Shit! I'm sorry," he said. "I should've left the room. I'm goin' now."

He headed toward the hallway that led to the kitchen.

"Hold up," Samn said, holding the bra in front of her breasts. "You've seen my tits before. I didn't think it'd be a big deal. I just feel better wearing runes, ya know?"

"Yes, I've seen them before," he said, still with his back to her, but no longer walking. "But that was 'cause I needed to. For medical reasons. You needed help. I don't need to see 'em now, and I'd like to respect your privacy."

He took another step, but startled when Samn placed a hand on his shoulder and spun him around. She let the bra she'd been holding over her breasts fall to the ground. Spider's eyes grew wide and he swallowed hard.

"What if I want you to look?" Samn said.

"Well, that's different," Spider said. "It's not that I don't wanna look. I just wanted to..."

Samn took a quick step toward him, startling him again. She took his face in her hands and pulled him into a firm kiss.

Spider held his hands up as if someone held a gun to his head, his eyes wide. He gave in, as if agreeing to die, and wrapped his arms around Samn. His rough hands pulled her close to him, his palms cold on her exposed flesh.

His hands roamed her back from shoulder blades to the top of her pants, creating electrifying friction.

She took his right hand and placed it on her left breast. Being aware of her injuries, he didn't squeeze, instead gently caressing the breast, allowing his thumb to occasionally graze the skin.

He pulled away from her, leaned down and placed a gentle kiss on her left breast. He kissed all around the nipple, careful to avoid the repaired incision, and then placed a final kiss on the nipple.

Samn leaned her head back and moaned. His lips felt incredible! She wanted them everywhere.

When Spider stood back up, she lifted his shirt over his head. Tattoos covered his torso: elaborate crescent moons circling each nipple, a sun with tentacle-like rays beaming off of it around his navel, and a ruby dragon circling his body from hip to shoulder. The dragon had an open scroll tucked into the bend of its body along Spider's left ribs. The scroll contained writing in a language Samn didn't understand.

She made a mental note to ask about it later, and began kissing his chest, feeling his hands in her hair.

Her hands roamed his body and landed on the firmness in his pants. Spider drew in a deep breath followed by a long exhale as Samn rubbed his cock.

She unbuckled his pants and dropped them to the floor. She always found it awkward when guys stumble around with their pants around their ankles, as if the looming prospect of sex had removed all logic from their brains, to the point that they'd forgotten that pants come off one leg at a time. She braced herself for the awkward moment, but Spider did not deliver. He stepped fluidly out of his pants, removing socks in the process, and stood naked before her.

Samn kissed him again and worked his penis in slow strokes from tip to balls. Spider's hands roamed her body, taking care to avoid aggravating any bandaged wounds.

Samn dropped to her knees and planted one kiss on his stomach before taking his penis into her mouth. She moved her lips back and forth along the shaft, allowing her tongue to swirl around the tip each time she reached the top. Spider's legs shook and he grabbed the edge of the record player to steady himself.

For once in her life, Samn felt safe during a sexual encounter. She'd never been with a guy who seemed to think before he fucked.

Spider lifted her and eased her onto her back, unbuttoned her pants and slid them off. He ran his hands up her legs, which were chilled and speckled with goosebumps. He hooked his fingers over the waist of her panties and slowly pulled them down.

A wave of self-consciousness washed over Samn. She hadn't shaved, well, anything in days, especially her vagina, which she typically only shaved when she stayed over at Brad's.

Brad's voice flooded her ears: "I am not licking that. Too much hair! It's fucking gross, babe. Shave that thing next time."

Did he really have her that trained? To ask how high when he says jump?

As thoughts raced through her head, she felt her panties slide past her feet. Spider cast them aside and licked her thigh, ending with a firm french kiss on her clit.

Samn moaned and arched her back as he worked his tongue up and down, in and out of her slit. He placed a finger inside her and her head spun, filling the empty house with cries of pleasure.

Spider crawled on top of her and gazed into her eyes.

"You sure you wanna do this?"

Samn smiled, nodded. "Yes! I've never been so sure." She kissed him.

"One sec," he said, and got up and crept out of the room, his rock-hard cock pointing straight ahead, not swinging like a pendulum.

Samn lay on her back alone on the cool floor, absently stroking her pussy, not wanting to lose this fire.

Spider returned with a pillow, a blanket and a condom.

"Safety and comfort first," he said, placing the pillow and blanket next to Samn.

She placed her head on the pillow and it smelled like Spider. He placed the condom on his dick and resumed his place on top of her, pulling the blanket with him.

"You still sure?" he said, his cock hovering inches from her entrance.

"Yes!" she said. "Fuck me! Please."

She grabbed his ass and pulled him into her, gasping as all seven inches slid inside.

He slid in and out of her gently at first, and then faster, harder. She felt his breath on her neck in between kisses, heard his moans in her ear. Samn wrapped her arms around him and held him tightly to her body as his hips continued to thrust and his hands roamed her body.

She expected the feelings of safety to leave, but they didn't. She was content, even happy, beneath Spider. She smiled and kissed his neck and cheek.

As her moans intensified, Spider withdrew his dick. *Here it cums*, Samn thought, consciously misspelling the word as she prepared for the blast. *Do all guys just want to cum in girls' mouths? I blame porn.*

But to her surprise, Spider turned his attention to her, aggressively rubbing her clit towards climax. Samn clutched the blanket, her dam about to burst, and then held her breath as she came. Short bursts of air escaped her lungs as the climax came to a close, and then Spider inserted himself inside of her once more.

Samn's legs felt boneless as Spider lifted them onto his shoulders and thrust himself deep inside her. She reached out her hand and he grasped it, kissed her knuckles, looked into her eyes and smiled.

His body shuddered and he released her legs, falling into her embrace. He moaned and trembled, clutched her shoulders, buried his face in her hair.

When he exhaled, it was a long, relaxed breath that smelled like cinnamon. He pulled out of her and rolled onto his back, sharing the same pillow with her. She settled her head onto his chest and he pulled the blanket around them.

"I think that's the first time I've ever orgasmed with a partner," she said.

"What? Get the fuck outta here?" he said. "What sort of asshole doesn't understand the concept of 'ladies first?'"

If you only knew, she thought. *If you only knew.*

Chapter 16

Return of the Pussy Pounder

Samn woke to a dark room, lit only by the blinding glow of her cellphone. She rolled away from Spider's chest where she had fallen asleep and retrieved the phone from where it buzzed on the floor.

"Brad calling…" the screen informed her.

"Shit," she said, her finger hovering over the "ignore" button. But she pressed the green answer button instead. "Hello?" she mumbled, her voice full of sleep.

"Look, I know it's late as fuck," Brad said, voice alert and anxious, "but have you seen Samn? I can't get a hold of her. I've been calling and calling and she won't answer."

"This is Samn, Brad!" she said, clearly annoyed.

"Samn? What the fuck? Where have you been? Why are you on Mandy's phone?"

Mandy's phone? she thought, her mind struggling to remove the last cobwebs of sleep. *Right, Mandy's phone!*

"It's a long story," Samn said. "Mandy's dead."

"Well, where are you? I've been worried sick. I'm sorry I got so pissed at dinner the other day. I think you should come over so we can talk it out."

"Did you not hear me, asshole?" Samn shouted, startling Spider awake. He sat upright and searched the room, reaching for one of the rune knives. "Mandy is fucking dead and all you can think about is getting back together?"

"Get back together? What do you mean? We never broke up!" A moment passed where neither of them spoke. "Wait, did you say Mandy is dead?"

"Yes, she is dead!" Samn shouted just before bursting into tears.

"What happened? Are you ok?"

As if you care, Samn thought. *You just want me to come over because you're fucking horny.*

"Long story short, the thing living in my boob killed her. And a bunch of other people too. It almost killed me." Her voice trailed off.

"That again?" He scoffed, stifled a laugh. "You must think I'm such a fucking idiot. You're probably in bed with the asshole who 'fixed your titty,'" he mocked.

Samn cast a guilty glance at Spider and could not meet his gaze. At least Brad was only half right. They weren't in bed. They'd had tremendous, unexpected sex on the floor!

"Look, Brad. I don't care what you think anymore. We're done. Don't call me."

"Is that little slut, Mandy, in bed with you too? Just how many people have you been fucking around with?"

"Mandy's in the fucking morgue!" Samn shouted, tears streaming down her face. "Don't you dare talk about her that way!"

"You were fucking easy to get into bed," Brad said. "We only dated, what? Like, two weeks before you were butt naked and sucking my dick? Fucking slut."

"Well, what does that make you? It takes two, you know!"

"It's different for guys. We're expected to have lots of sex. Girls are just whores. Sluts. Pieces of ass."

He was trying to get a rise out of her and she knew it. She could smell the trap. She didn't fall for it. Instead, she said: "well, if girls are such whores, I guess all you acceptably sex-crazed boys will just have to fuck each other!"

She smashed her thumb into the hang-up button, and heard Brad shouting into the phone as the call ended. She hung her head and sobbed.

Spider slid close to her and placed an arm around her shoulder.

"You alright?" he said.

"How much of that did you hear?" she said, staring at the floor.

"Dude was bein' pretty loud. To be honest with ya, I heard a lot."

"Fuck! You must think I'm awful." She rolled her eyes, cursing Brad for leaving one last ruinous impact on her life.

"Naw," he said. "Quite the opposite. I think you're a damn fine woman. That fella was way outta line."

Her eyes bore into him, asking a thousand silent questions.

"I'm a slut!" he laughed. "If that's what that fella wants to call it. I found a nice girl that I like a lot. Hopped right in bed with her without hesitation. No regrets."

Samn laughed.

"Sex is part of being human," he said, tilting his forehead until it touched hers. "Shouldn't feel guilty about it. That's like feelin' guilty for eatin' or breathin'."

"Hold me," she said, forcing thoughts of Mandy's body at the morgue from her mind.

They resumed their position wrapped in the blanket, Spider flat on his back, Samn's head on his chest. Moments later, sleep claimed them.

Chapter 17
A Plan to Save the Titties

Samn painted the last bullets with runes, loaded the pistol, and placed the rest, save one, back in the container. Spider picked up the remaining bullet and examined the tiny rune.

"Not bad," he said. "Tiny, but spot on."

The rune, painted with a thin-bristled brush, was squat and rounder than normal--out of necessity, being painted along the bullet's tip--but was easily discernible as the same character.

"You really think those things will come after me again?" Samn said.

"Maybe not all of 'em, but definitely the one that's used to ya."

"I'm pretty sure that one's dead," she said. "I stabbed it with a scalpel. The last time I saw the little bastard, the scalpel was still hanging out of it and its blood was all over the floor."

"Accordin' to Shadowcub, they're pretty tough. Maybe it's dead. Maybe it ain't. I'm just sayin', best to be ready for 'im."

Samn crossed her arms over her chest, remembering the last few days with startling clarity.

"So, do we just wait for it to show up?"

"No," Spider said. "We're goin' huntin'."

The old Camaro hummed along the interstate. Samn's body rumbled along with the car's high-speed vibrato. Despite the car's age and the exterior lacking paint, the interior sported lush, clean carpet, painted accents along the dash, and newly upholstered seats. Samn barely recognized the car during the day with bright sunlight streaming through the windows.

Spider clicked the right signal and merged into the exit lane towards Samn's apartment. She needed a change of clothes, and they figured her apartment was the best place to begin their hunt, considering the creature's familiarity with it.

Spider pulled the Camaro into a vacant parking spot in front of Samn's building and shut off the engine. Samn stared up to the second floor at the front window of her kitchen, eyes squinted and searching for any form of movement.

"You sure you're good to go in there?" Spider said, picking up on Samn's tension. "I don't care one bit to head on up, grab ya some clothes and check the place out."

"I'm good," Samn said, still not taking her eyes off the window. "Can't be afraid forever."

Spider smiled. "Right on."

Samn exited the vehicle and followed Spider to the landing and up the stairs. Spider crept up the stairs with slow, deliberate strides. Samn's eyes shifted back and forth between his ass and the pistol tucked into the back of his jeans. She was damned glad he was here, for multiple reasons.

"Door's still locked," he said.

"Well, I didn't expect the little fuckers to pick the lock and go in the old fashioned way." Samn smiled, but it didn't last long. "I guess my key is back at Mandy's place. Shit!"

"No problem," Spider said. He dropped to one knee and pulled a pair of bobby pins from his pocket. "Never let a locked door stand in your way." He grinned and inserted the pins into the lock. Seconds later, he turned the door knob and the door swung open.

"Terrifying," Samn said matter-of-factly. "Who knew it's always been that easy to break into my apartment?"

"Get a deadbolt," Spider said. "Not impossible to pick, but a whole lot harder."

Spider crept inside and Samn followed. She surveyed the apartment and found it just as she'd left it. She pulled the lock-back knife from her pocket, opened it and held it in front of her.

"I'll check the bedroom," Samn said. "Get some clothes while I'm in there."

"Alright. I'll poke around in here. Holler if you see anything weird."

Samn tiptoed to the ajar bedroom door and pushed it open. The hinges groaned and caused Samn to shiver. Leaving the door open, just in case, she snuck along the room's perimeter and checked along the baseboard, behind the curtains, and along the window sill. Nothing.

Brandishing the knife in her right hand, she pulled the blanket from the bed with her left and let it fall to the floor. She held her breath, expecting to see dozens of writhing papillasites beneath, but instead saw nothing but clean sheets.

A clatter from the kitchen shattered the silence, startling Samn. She whirled around and held the knife in front of her in both hands, eyes wide and searching the floor.

"Who the hell are you?" A familiar voice, but not Spider's.

"Friend, I'll thank ya to keep yer hands off o' me."

Oh shit! Samn thought. *Brad, don't you dare fuck this up! I finally found a guy who treats me like a person. You stay the fuck away from him. And me!*

She ran to the kitchen to find Brad standing over Spider, who had fallen back into a loaded dish drainer. Spider held his hands up as if at gunpoint, even though he was the only one with a weapon. Brad fumed, chested heaving, nostrils flared.

"Samn! Who the fuck is this...thing?" Brad said.

"Brad, calm down."

"Like hell! I knew you were fucking somebody else, but I never expected it to be somebody like this." He gestured to Spider in disgust. "I always knew you liked devil music and what not, but deep down I always thought you were better than that."

Samn hung her head, shoulders slumped.

"We're done, Brad. Remember? Who and what I do are my business. Not yours." She tried to put her anger into these words, but it didn't work. The anger filled the words like a balloon with a small hole somewhere and came across exhausted.

"We're not done," Brad said. "That's a decision both of us have to make, and I say we're still a thing. So, get rid of this fucking guy so we can talk."

Samn locked eyes with Spider, who motioned towards the door in a want-me-to-go gesture. Samn shook her head. "No," she mouthed.

"Hey! Look at me, bitch! Not him!" Brad shouted.

He grabbed Samn's chin and spun her head to look at him.

"That'll be about enough o' that," Spider said. "I'm content to wait outside if Samn wants to talk to ya, but I won't sit here and watch you rough her up."

"Brad, let me go!" Samn said, the words muffled by her contorted lips. He squeezed harder, his fingernails digging into her bottom lip. She tasted blood.

The anger filled her, replacing exhaustion with rage. *Who the fuck does he think he is?*

She pushed him, causing him to stumble, but he didn't release her face. He regained his footing and clutched her face in both hands.

"Alright, fuck you, buddy," Spider said, placing the gun on the countertop. He took two steps towards Brad, but before he could act, Samn balled her fist and swung hard at Brad's jaw.

He reeled, releasing her face and toppling over backward, falling flat on his ass.

"Damn!" Spider said, smiling. "Remind me never to piss you off."

Samn smiled despite her throbbing hand. She locked eyes with Brad and the smile vanished.

"Don't you ever put your fucking hands on me again!" she said, eyes narrowed, voice booming.

Brad shook his head and squinted. He rose to his feet using the counter to steady himself. His lips quivered, teeth clenched, and a low growl escaped his throat. He lunged at Samn and wrapped both hands around her throat.

"You don't get to fucking hit me, you slut!"

He slapped her repeatedly. Samn's vision went completely dark from the impact, and then the darkness slowly dissipated revealing bright white with vibrant red along the edges.

Samn heard Spider's voice, but it was faint, distant, drowned out by the ringing in her ears.

"That's enough o' that, I said!"

Spider pulled Brad off of Samn and clocked him with a closed fist. Spider cocked his hand back to hit him again, but Brad crumpled to the floor, blood oozing from his nose.

"You alright?" Spider said, kneeling next to Samn. "Sorry I got involved. I don't like to meddle, but that fella was outta hand."

Samn's vision cleared just in time to see Brad looming over Spider, a skillet held high.

"Look out!" Samn shouted, but it was too late.

The skillet pinged off Spider's head and he collapsed on top of her. Brad rolled him to the side, his body limp and climbed on top of Samn.

"How could you do this to us?" he shouted. "We were happy! I was good to you! And you fucking cheat on me with some goth-ass redneck?"

You were happy, Samn thought, tried to say, but the words didn't come out.

"And you're wearing his fucking clothes?" Brad took hold of Samn's oversized black T in both hands and tugged. The shirt tore down the middle, revealing Samn's torso, the painted rune bra still hanging in place by one shoulder strap.

"What the fuck is this?" Brad said, snatching the bra between the cups. The elastic snapped her back and the bra tore free. Brad held it up like a trophy. "Did he paint this shit on your underwear? Samn, what the fuck have you gotten into? You're better than this. We were better than this!"

Samn tried to cover her breasts with her hands, but Brad pinned them to the floor, a tight grasp on each wrist.

He eyed her breasts in horror and a tear came to his eye.

"What did he do to you?"

He released Samn's right hand and caressed the repaired wounds on Samn's breast.

Samn shuddered, as if Brad's fingers were roaming insects. Tears brimmed her eyes and her heartbeat thudded in her chest like a war drum.

She lunged at Brad's wrist that still held her left arm, sinking her teeth into the flesh. She snarled and rejoiced as her mouth filled with Brad's blood, as if something primal had awakened deep within her.

Brad howled in pain and released her wrist. He pulled the wounded wrist to his chest, snatching it from between Samn's clenched teeth, tearing flesh free. He stared at her in disbelief and horror, as if watching a helpless damsel suddenly transform into a blood-starved beast.

Brad lifted his hand to strike her again, but Samn plunged her thumbs into both of his eyes. He recoiled and fell off of her, squinting, trying to regain his vision.

"Don't you fucking touch me!" Samn snarled.

Brad tackled her out of desperation, out of fear. He pinned her back to the ground, crying, as if hating himself for what he prepared to do to her.

Samn growled and flailed like a rabid animal, but Brad was too heavy, his sports-trained muscles too strong.

A buzzing, humming, tapping joined the war drum in Samn's chest. Her wide, panicked eyes darted from Brad's contorted face to her thrumming breast. Her rage faded and fear took over as a trail of insects burst forth from her nipple, one after the other, and marched in a line down the mound of her breast and onto her stomach.

"What the fuck?" Brad screamed, releasing her and backing away.

But he wasn't quick enough. Several of the creatures had crawled onto his clothes. Samn swatted the bugs off her stomach and sat up, watching as four of them marched along Brad's jacket, some heading north, some heading south.

"Samn, what the fuck are those things?" he cried.

Screams soon replaced his cries, as two of the creatures entered his trousers and two worked their way up his neck.

Samn looked closer at the ones she had swatted from her stomach. They looked like ants at a glance, but upon closer examination, she saw that they were tiny papillasites.

That fucking thing gave birth in my tit! Samn thought.

She snatched the rune bra off the floor where Brad had dropped it and cupped it over her breasts, half afraid of what else might have escaped, half afraid of what might try to go back inside.

Brad screamed, swatting at his crotch, and then his neck. Two tiny streams of blood ran down his neck and pooled at his collar. The swats seem to have no effect on the creatures.

Panic-stricken, Brad unbuckled his belt and unbuttoned his pants, dropping them with shaking hands. Blood coated his partially erect dick, and in the midst of the blood, Samn spotted two tiny papillasites, clawing and biting. One of them crawled up the slippery shaft and burrowed inside of Brad's urethra.

Brad writhed in pain, clawing at his neck, holding the head of his penis. He screamed, cried, fell to the floor and stared at his penis in horror.

The penis split open like a peeled banana, the flesh splitting with the peel, revealing the growing papillasite feasting on the ruined stump. Brad screamed, screamed, and then fell silent as the creatures continued to eat, tearing holes in his crotch and neck. His body fell limp and all light left his eyes.

Samn clutched the rune bra to her chest and surveyed the bloody kitchen, searching for her knife. Her eyes darted to Brad's papillasites which had yet to notice her, but she had lost sight of the others.

She continued her search, crawling around the kitchen, desperate to find the knife. The blade protruded from beneath Spider's unconscious body. At first, Samn thought it had stabbed him—there was certainly enough blood—but the blade was clearly visible, not sticking into his flesh.

She grabbed the blade, her hand slick from crawling through blood, her other hand struggling to hold the rune bra in place. Eventually, it pulled free but nicked Samn's finger. She winced, but did not release the blade, instead positioning it in her hand properly. She crawled back towards Brad's body, the papillasites still intent on their meal, and slashed at the creatures—now a couple inches tall at least—still devouring Brad's scrotum.

The blade swung high at the first attempt and drew the attention of the monster. It glared at her, its fangs and nails still dripping with gore. It crawled out of the split penis towards her, but before it could regain its footing, Samn slashed again, this time connecting with the thing's torso, splitting it in half.

The glowing red eyes dimmed and then went out as the creature's halves toppled down Brad's balls and onto the floor.

Samn lunged at the second creature, which snacked contently on the tender flesh where Brad's balls met the imploded shaft of his penis. The blade connected, severing the thing's head.

She crawled toward the papillasites on Brad's neck and stabbed at them, missing. The creatures--nowhere near as big as the others--didn't seem to notice the blade sinking into Brad's neck. Samn drew the blade out and stabbed again. This strike cut one of the creatures, but not enough to kill it. The creature wailed and turned its attention to Samn.

Panicked, Samn stabbed again and again. And again. Some of the strikes hit home, but all sank into Brad's flesh causing fresh blood to pool. Samn raised the knife and brought it down repeatedly, the creatures' blood mixing with Brad's as it spattered Samn's face and chest.

She screamed! And then realized that she knew the creatures had died, but continued to stab anyway.

Brad, you piece of shit. I think you finally made me cum.

Samn sat with her back against the wall, knife held in one hand, rune bra pressed to her chest with the other. She searched the room for movement, fearful that the other creatures would return any moment to feast, grow and then attempt to burrow back into her boob for a nap.

When movement came, Samn tensed and pointed the trembling blade at the source. She saw no papillasites, just the flutter of Spider's eyelids. He groaned and sat up holding his head.

"What the fuck hit me?" he said. Blinking rapidly, he surveyed the room in horror. "What the fuck happened in here?"

Samn waddled toward him on her knees, still awkwardly clutching the runes to her chest. She buried her face in his jacket and began to sob.

Spider wrapped his arms around her and stroked her hair, which was matted with sticky blood.

"Easy," he said. "Just tell me what happened. Are you ok?"

"That thing had babies," Samn stammered, "in me. Brad tore my bra off and they came out! They killed him." She sobbed and drew ragged breaths. "I killed the four that were on Brad, but the rest got away. They were so tiny! Are they coming back?"

Spider examined Brad's body, his eyes drifting from shredded penis to multiple stab wounds in his neck.

"Prob'ly will," he said, his voice distant and monotone. "What happened to 'is neck?"

Samn leaned back and held Spider's gaze, eyes wet with tears.

"I missed." She wiped her eyes with the heel of her hand. "And then I didn't. I just kept stabbing and stabbing even after those things were dead. I've never been a violent person, but he treated me like shit for so long. Today, he crossed a line." She sniffed and closed her eyes. When they opened, her eyes narrowed, brow furrowed. "He beat me today. I'm pretty sure he was going to rape me. He ripped my clothes off and put his hands on me. Stabbing him felt just as good as, no, probably better than stabbing those creatures."

Spider's eyes widened. Samn's pulse hammered in her veins.

Am I insane? she thought. *Have I lost my mind? Was he still alive? Did I murder Brad? Is Spider afraid of me now? Am I afraid of me?*

Spider whistled. "That's fucked up," he chuckled. "I'm damn sorry he knocked me out. And even sorrier that all that fucked up shit happened to you. Fucker got what he deserved."

Spider extended a leg and kicked Brad's foot.

"So, the rune knife worked, yeah?"

Samn nodded. "Cut right through them."

Spider stood, massaging his temples, and helped Samn to her feet. She took both of Spider's hands and the bra fell to the floor. Panicked, she stooped, retrieved it and pressed it firmly to her chest.

"I need a new rune bra," she said, laughing.

"Want me to fetch ya one?"

"Please," she said, leaning on the kitchen counter for support. "My bedroom is at the end of the hall."

Spider stumbled down the hallway, swaying on his feet as though drunk. *Brad really whacked him. I hope he's ok.*

Moments later, he returned with a red cotton bra in hand.

"This work?" he said.

"Yeah," Samn said, taking the garment from his out-stretched hand. He placed a bottle of black nail polish on the counter next to her.

Samn started painting the backwards runes on the cups of the bra.

"You know, this gives me a hell of an idea," she said, licking her lips and leaning close to the painted letters. "You know any good tattoo artists?"

Spider guffawed and clapped his hands together. "I do! She even specializes in occult imagery." He beamed at her. "If you're goin' where I think you are."

Samn smiled back and returned her attention to the task at hand.

She finished the runes over the next ten minutes, carefully minding each detail. She blew the nail polish to make sure it was dry and then admired her handy work.

"Look accurate?" she asked.

"Aye," Spider said. "That'll keep 'em out."

She slipped her arms into the bra and went to fasten it, wincing at fresh pain in her shoulder.

"Can you give me a hand with this?"

Spider approached her, fastened the bra. He kissed her shoulder. One gentle peck.

"This may be the worst timing a man's ever had," he said. "But..." He trailed off. "Ah, never mind."

"Say what you were going to say," Samn said, peering at him over her shoulder, still cherishing the warmth of his lips on her cold skin. Spider protested, blushing. "I've had a shitty day," she said. "Out with it."

"Well, I'll gladly be yours if you'd like to be mine." He held her gaze despite his obvious bashfulness.

"You mean like *go steady*?" Samn said in a mocking voice.

"Aye," he said. "Somethin' like that. Boyfriend and girlfriend. Whatever ye wanna call it."

"I call it a damn good idea," she said, and kissed him. The kiss was long and passionate, tasted of cinnamon. She eased away from him, her lips longing for more, but there would be plenty of time for that later.

Spider grinned that sly, crooked grin. *The* grin.

"And your timing couldn't be better," she said, wrapping her right arm around his neck. "My ex is definitely out of the picture now." She giggled.

"Holy shit!" Spider said, laughing. "That's so wrong."

"Too soon?"

"Way too soon! Can't be joking about a dead man while his body's still warm."

"If I didn't laugh about it, I'd just end up crying again."

She rested her head on his chest, felt his gentle heartbeat thumping beneath her ear.

"No more jokes," she said. "But if we're going to date, I have just one rule."

"Yeah? What's 'at?"

She glanced at Brad's corpse and then back to Spider, wearing a mischievous grin.

"Never ask me about my body count."

Epilogue

Samn lay on the tattoo table, wincing occasionally, as Shadowcub etched backwards runes into the skin around her nipples. Spider sat across from her leaned back in a chair, ankles crossed, hands behind his head.

"I must say," Shadowcub said, "applying the runes backward to your bra was genius."

"I was tired of seeing shit pop out of my tits," Samn said, eyes locked on the ceiling. "My titties, my rules."

Samn and Spider had been questioned thoroughly by the police, but it helped their case that they called them willingly, and that their stories matched not only each other's, but were consistent with papillasite footage at the hospital. The cops had asked Samn about the knife wounds in Brad's neck and chest and she admitted to putting them there, although completely post-mortem and by consequence of trying to kill the tiny creatures.

Spider's story matched Samn's despite them being questioned separately, and just like that, Samn and Spider were free to go, but the sheriff asked them to please "not leave town."

"Your first tattoo, and you get it around your nipples," Spider said. "Don't get me wrong, I get why. But girl, you're way more metal than me."

Samn looked at him and smiled, thankful that his comments were complimentary and not damning. She could get used to a guy who respected her decisions and didn't treat her tits like a dirty secret. First time for everything.

"It's not so bad," Samn said, sucking air through her teeth and wincing from new pain.

"Not so bad, huh?" Shadowcub said, smiling. "So, what's the plan?"

"Well, I figure we'll fuck a lot, but we haven't quite set a date yet," Samn said. Spider howled with laughter.

"Not what I meant," Shadowcub said, sitting up from the tattoo and running a hand through her short black hair. "I mean, what about them?"

"Them?" Spider asked.

"You know what I'm talking about. I've never heard of such an infestation."

"I figure, after what happened at the hospital, the proper authorities will handle it," Samn said, examining her breasts and nodding approval of the half-finished tattoos.

"My dear," Shadowcub said, "this is not the first time paranormal creatures have caused a public stir, but it always gets explained away. Those news reports next week will change their tone. Maybe the footage was tampered with, an immature joke. Oh, this just in, the murders committed at the hospital were not tiny monsters, but instead the work of an underground cult. Things like that. I assure you, the authorities are busier right now rationalizing this to the press than they are hunting papillasites."

"You've got to be kidding me!" Samn said, propping herself up on her elbows.

"Afraid not," Spider said.

"Welcome to the club," Shadowcub added. "Lay back down and let's get these runes finished."

Samn resumed her place on the table. "What club?"

"The occultists' club of solitude and disappointment," Shadowcub said, smiling as she turned her attention back to Samn's breasts. "No matter what happens, we are in this alone and our work is always undervalued and underappreciated. By the masses, that is. People just can't wrap their heads around what they don't understand."

"You make this club sound so appealing," Samn said.

"It ain't all bad," Spider said. "We meet some cool people and get to help 'em. Make decent money at it too."

"Then I guess there are a lot of women right now who need our help," Samn said. "Judging by what happened at the hospital."

"That is correct," Shadowcub said. "I've already put a bulletin up on the website, attempting to get an early rebuke of the sure-to-come downplay on the news. And I've scheduled an appointment to get my boobs done."

"You're getting a boob job?" Samn said. "At a time like this?"

"Not a boob job," Shadowcub said, rolling her eyes. "Tattoos. I have a feeling this is going to be a popular one."

"Wow," Samn joked. "I've never been a trend setter before."

The sun had set by the time Shadowcub proclaimed the tattoos completed. She sat back and admired them.

"That's some great work, SC," Spider said. "Runes are perfect. That'll keep the little bastards out."

Samn found it odd that she felt less naked now, with everyone in the room staring at her exposed tits, than she had ever felt in the past with guys like Brad. The runes still stung, but made her feel safe.

"Come on over to the mirror and check them out," Shadowcub said.

Samn got up from the table and followed Shadowcub to a tall mirror. She examined her boobs and found it pleasant to no longer view them as a problem. They were perky and secure, and the tattoos diminished the scarring considerably. Samn absently poked at the scar where Spider had extracted the sleeping creature, the rough, discolored skin standing in contrast to the smooth flesh surrounding it.

"Wait a minute!" Samn said. "What if we have proof?"

"Proof of what?" Shadowcub asked. "Of papillasites?"

"Yeah!" Samn said.

"We already have video footage from the hospital, but I'm sure that will conveniently disappear and get explained away. What could be better than that?"

"Two things," Samn said. "My doctor ordered a mammogram before those babies busted out of me. I bet it'll show them! And I'm willing to bet that Dr. Sprake is not the type of doctor to explain away pressing medical concerns."

Shadowcub considered this.

"That may work," she said. "But you'll need to get to the good doctor and the mammogram results before the 'authorities' do."

"Sounds like we have a goal," Spider said. "I love goals."

Samn wrapped both of her arms around his neck and stood on tip-toes to kiss him.

"Get down now," Shadowcub said, eyes wide and voice trembling. She pressed two fingers into each of her temples and winced. "Now!"

She flung her tiny frame at Samn and Spider, knocking the unexpectant couple to the ground, just as the front window of the tattoo parlor shattered and a projectile entered the room. The tiny silver object whizzed over Shadowcub's head and stuck in the back wall.

"What the fuck was that?" Spider said.

"I don't know, but I could sense it coming," Shadowcub said, still massaging her temples.

Samn got to her feet and approached the silver object: a scalpel, discolored with dried, black papillasite blood.

Samn peered from the scalpel to the broken window and could have sworn she saw faint yellow eyes in the darkness.

"Fuck," she said. "Someone doesn't like my new tattoos."